LOVE RENEWED

A SECOND CHANCE WITH YOU

LORANA HOOPES

For my Family who lets me write.
To the other Second Chance authors. It was amazing working with you.
To my amazing readers, thank you for picking up this book. Please leave a review.

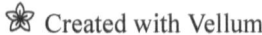

NOTE FROM THE AUTHOR

Thank you so much for picking up this book. I hope you enjoy the story and the characters as they are dear to my heart. If you do, please leave a review at your retailer. It really does make a difference because it lets people make an informed decision about books. I'd also like to offer you a sample of my newest book. This will sign you up for my newsletter which allows me to send you weekly emails with news and promotional information about my books, but you are welcome to cancel any time. Free Sample!

Sign up for Lorana Hoopes's newsletter and get her book, The Billionaire's Impromptu Bet, as a welcome gift. Get Started Now!

Lorana's Billionaire Books:

The Billionaire's Secret

Brush With a Billionaire

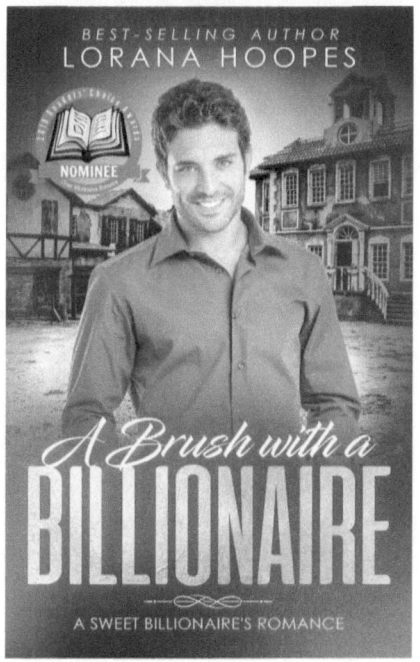

The Billionaire's Christmas Miracle

The Billionaire's Cowboy Groom

The Cowboy Billionaire Coming Soon!

BEST-SELLING AUTHOR
LORANA HOOPES

The
COWBOY
Billionaire

A SWEET BILLIONAIRES ROMANCE

CHAPTER 1

M rs. Kaitlyn Fields. Seventeen year old Kaitlyn scribbled the name again and again in her notebook. At least three pages were filled with the name and several more with her plans for their life together: wedding colors, children's names, places they would live.

"You've got it bad," her friend Tiffany teased as she spied the notebook.

"I can't help it." Kaitlyn sighed. "I just know we're going to get married someday."

"I bet you guys do. You are such a cute couple. Do you think he'll give you his senior ring?" Tiffany lifted up part of her crimped hair, pulling it into a scrunchie.

Kaitlyn smiled and closed the notebook. "I think he's

going to tonight. I know he picked it up at school yesterday, and it would be perfect timing tonight at homecoming."

"I'm so jealous of you," Tiffany said, "but in a good way."

"Don't worry." Kaitlyn wrapped an arm around her friend's shoulder. "I'm sure you'll find your Prince Charming soon."

Kaitlyn stared at the date on the calendar. Had it really been a year? Of course it felt much longer. She had left three years ago when Jack was just two; he barely remembered his father, but the divorce hadn't been finalized until last year.

"Hey, you okay?"

Kaitlyn looked up to see Melody Phelps, her best friend and business partner, in the doorway. She shook her head. "Yeah, I was just caught off guard by the date. My divorce was finalized a year ago today."

Sympathy flooded Melody's blue eyes. "Oh, I'm so sorry, Kaitlyn."

Kaitlyn shrugged. "It's better this way, believe me, but it's still hard."

"I'm afraid I don't have good news either." Melody waved the piece of paper in her hand. "Quarterly reports. We need a good job quickly or we're going to have to do something drastic." She handed the reports to Kaitlyn and then shuffled out of the office.

Kaitlyn sighed as she reviewed them. More money was definitely going out than coming in, and they would need to turn it around soon or they would lose the business. She had thought interior decorating would be easy, but it was proving a challenge to get noticed and even harder to get booked. Of course that probably had a lot to do with her personality. She had always been on the shyer side around people she didn't know, but she was a great designer. If only she could find a way to get clients coming to her.

Beside her, the phone rang and Kaitlyn picked it up without even glancing at the caller ID. "Kaitlyn Bell Designs."

"Hi Kaitlyn. This is Margie Fields."

Kaitlyn gripped the phone tighter and sat up straighter even though the woman on the other end couldn't see her. What could the mother of her ex-boyfriend want? "Uh, hi Margie, what can I do for you?"

"Well, I heard through the grapevine that you were a decorator. You always did have an eye for design. Anyway, I don't know if you remember, but we own a lodge in the mountains and the main room needs to be redone. I was hoping you might be able to work some magic on it before the Christmas season."

How could Kaitlyn forget the lodge in the mountains? It had been her home away from home every Christmas in high school as her dad often traveled for work. She hated that he was gone most holidays, but Dillon's family had taken her in with open arms. She had fond memories of skiing there, building snowmen with Dillon, and then cuddling by the fire.

But there was the rub. All the memories of the place included Dillon. Dillon, whom she thought she was going to marry, but who had left town after high school to explore the world while Kaitlyn stayed close to home. Kaitlyn bit her lip as she pondered the offer. She needed the work and the money, but what if Dillon would be there? Could she handle seeing him again?

"Oh, and if you were worried about Dillon, he won't be there. I'll be there of course and we'll have some guests, but they can avoid the room you're working in."

"Oh, I wasn't," Kaitlyn stammered, but there was nothing to say. Margie had read her mind. Again. She'd had a knack for knowing what was on Kaitlyn's mind whenever they had conversed when Kaitlyn was in high school, and it appeared she hadn't lost her touch. Kaitlyn had once loved that trait about her as Margie had filled the gaping hole of Kaitlyn's mother who had died when she was thirteen. Kaitlyn took a deep breath and started again. "I'd love to, Margie, but before Christmas? That's only two weeks away."

"I know, and I apologize, but I just found out the lodge was picked to be in a travel magazine, and they are coming two days before Christmas to photograph it. That means I need the room redone and decorated for Christmas by the twenty-third. I can pay you handsomely."

"I'll have to make sure everything is available locally then. We won't have time to order."

"That's fine, and again, we can pay for expedited shipping if we need to."

Kaitlyn bit her lip and did a quick calculation. She would need to hire a crew. There was no way she and Melody would be able to finish by themselves in that time. "It won't be cheap, Margie, but would you like to meet up and discuss designs?"

"Yes, dear, I'd love to. Do you have an office?"

"Absolutely," Kaitlyn rattled off her address and set a date for a meeting before hanging up the phone.

"Did I hear that right?" Melody asked appearing again in her doorway. Her blue eyes were wide with surprise. Kaitlyn and Melody had met at design school and while Kaitlyn preferred decorating homes, Melody preferred doing businesses. Between the two of them, they made a dynamic duo and Kaitlyn loved her. But Melody had one annoying habit. The ability to always hear everything. "Did you just agree to do work for Margie Fields?"

"I did." Kaitlyn tucked a strand of dark hair behind her ears and pulled back her shoulders. "We need the money, and she will be good for business. Margie Fields is a big name."

"She is." Melody nodded and crossed her arms as she leaned against the doorframe. "But you sure this has nothing to do with Dillon?" Dillon had been out of the picture before she met Melody - off to make his mark in the world. However, after Melody tried to set Kaitlyn up on a few dates and Kaitlyn always reneged, Melody had probed into the reason. Kaitlyn had been forced to tell her the story of Dillon Fields, the man who broke her heart. And probably didn't even know it.

"No, Dillon won't even be there." Kaitlyn hated the heat that crawled across her face at the mention of Dillon. It had been ten years. Why did his very name still send her heart fluttering?

"Uh huh." Melody's brow arched and her frank gaze told Kaitlyn she wasn't buying it. "I still think you're playing with fire, but I guess you know best, boss." She shook her head before disappearing from the doorframe.

Kaitlyn sighed. She probably was playing with fire. She'd done everything she could to avoid even the thought of Dillon for almost a decade, Not that it had helped. Having always been shy, when Dillon left, her self-esteem had dropped even further, sending her into one bad relationship after another until she ended up marrying Jerry.

Things had been great for a year, but when she got pregnant, they spiraled quickly out of control. Since then, she had become even more withdrawn, dating very rarely and when she did, she compared every man she dated to Dillon, which was why few lasted past the first date. Now, she was basically walking into the lion's den. It didn't even matter that he wouldn't be there. Margie would remind her of him, and there was bound to be a lingering essence of him in the lodge. She would just have to make sure her walls were up. This was a job. Nothing more.

DILLON STARED at the array of rings in the case.

"Do you see something that you like?" The salesman, an immaculately dressed man in a blue suit, asked him from the other side of the counter.

"I'm not sure." He had thought this would be easy. After all, he loved Shana, didn't he? He certainly loved the idea of Shana. What wasn't to love about a supermodel girlfriend? But then why was he having such a hard time picking a ring?

The man raised an eyebrow. "Does the woman like round or princess cut diamonds?"

"Uh, I have no idea." Dillon had never looked too closely at Shana's hands. "Does that matter?"

"Depends on the woman. Some women do not care and some have very specific ideas of what they want to wear for the rest of their lives."

Shana definitely had specific ideas of what she wanted. At least when it came to clothing and food and vacation spots. So why did he not know her feelings about this?

He sighed. The rest of their lives. Those five words gave him pause. Did he really want to spend the rest of his life with Shana? Or was he proposing because they had been together for six months and everyone was telling him it was time?

"If you do not know, then why are you proposing to this woman?"

That was a good question. "I don't know," Dillon said shaking his head. "Thank you, my friend. I don't think I'll be buying a ring today, but you've definitely given me something to think about."

The man behind the counter nodded, and Dillon exited the shop. He walked down the sidewalk to a nearby coffee shop and ordered an Americano. Coffee in hand, he sat down at one of the tables and pondered his life. He was nearing thirty, and he wanted a family, so why was his throat drying up at the prospect of proposing to Shana? He'd had several relationships the last few years, and none of them had lasted. Did that mean something was wrong with him or was he simply dating the wrong women?

He sipped his coffee and watched the people pass by in shorts and t-shirts. It was December, but it sure didn't feel like it in Florida. And forget snow. He missed snow. Maybe it was time for a change of scenery.

CHAPTER 2

K aitlyn took a deep breath. Margie Fields was here. She needed this job. She would be professional. Pulling her shoulders back, she stood and smoothed her olive green pencil skirt. It had taken her twice as long to get ready this morning knowing Margie was coming today, but Kaitlyn thought the cream silk shirt and olive skirt worked.

"Hi, Margie. It's so good to see you again." Kaitlyn pasted on her professional face as she greeted the wealthy older woman, but her heart was hammering in her chest. How long had it been since she'd seen Dillon's mother? Probably around the time she and Dillon went their separate ways.

"It's good to see you too, dear." Margie stepped forward as if to hug her, then paused and extended her hand instead.

Kaitlyn shook it, glad the woman hadn't continued going for the hug. It had been too long.

Margie's grey hair was pulled up in an immaculate updo and her tailored pantsuit showed off her thin figure. Her hair had turned grey when Kaitlyn and Dillon were in high school, but somehow she managed to pull it off and look distinguished rather than just old. Kaitlyn, on the other hand, had to see her stylist once a month to keep her grey hairs covered up. She didn't have many, but they stuck out in her dark hair like icicles on a Christmas tree.

"Come into my conference room. I threw some ideas together after your email." Margie's email had come just hours after they had spoken on the phone and Kaitlyn had spent the next few days whipping up designs before this meeting.

Kaitlyn led the older woman past Melody's watchful eye and into the small conference room. The office space wasn't very big. It held Melody's desk, Kaitlyn's office, the conference room, a small kitchen, and an even smaller bathroom, but it worked for now.

"So, keeping your rustic theme in mind, I came up with three options for you, and of course, if you don't like any of them, I can make additional changes."

"I'm sure one of them will be fine," Margie said as she pulled out a chair and sat down. She folded her hands in her lap and looked up at the screen as she waited for Kaitlyn to begin.

Kaitlyn nodded, trying to calm her nerves. She clicked on the big screen that took up one wall in the room and opened her laptop before sitting next to Margie. The first picture filled the screen. It had the room decorated in dark browns and creams. A large brick fireplace held the focus in the main room underneath a large mounted deer head. The couches were brown leather and the Christmas tree was large and lit with white lights.

Margie tilted her head as she regarded the pictures. "It's beautiful but maybe a little too rustic. Women tend to be our biggest clientele, and I can't imagine the animal head would be a big seller."

Kaitlyn issued a nervous giggle and tucked a strand of hair behind her ear. "Of course we could easily remove that, but let me show you what else we have." She clicked the next button on her laptop and pictures of the room done in mauves and pale pinks filled the screen. An abstract painting replaced the mounted head. The tree in this one was flocked white with pink lights. This one was less rustic, but Kaitlyn had thrown it in because sometimes people said they wanted one thing but really wanted something different when they saw it.

That was not Margie though, as her forehead wrinkled slightly. "Again lovely, but not exactly what I had in mind."

"Don't worry. I saved the best for last," Kaitlyn said as she clicked the next button. She held her breath but was pleased when Margie's eyes lit up. For this one, she had decorated the room in hunter green and red. Traditional Christmas colors. Red and green striped pillows completed the beige colored couches and a beautiful landscape painting hung on the wall. White lights hung from the crown molding, and the tree was large and decorated with multicolored lights.

"Now this I love," Margie said. "It feels like home, and I love the wallpaper. I'm not normally a wallpaper fan, but only because I hate removing it."

Kaitlyn smiled. Removing old wallpaper was one of her least favorite things too, but a good wallpaper really brought life to a room. "Wonderful. Is there anything you want to change?"

Margie scanned the pictures again before shaking her head. "No, everything looks wonderful. How long do you think it will take?"

"Well, it depends on how much I have to take down and clear out, but once that is done, I think a week will be enough. I'm going to have to hire a crew though. Melody and I can't possibly do this on our own in that time."

"But it will be ready for the picture?" Margie's voice was full of hope.

"Yeah, if everything goes according to plan, I should be finished by the twenty-second. That will give you a day to get prepared."

"This is wonderful, Kaitlyn. I knew you would be perfect for this job."

Kaitlyn smiled. She was glad Margie had liked the designs and even more pleased to be working again. Even better, this job would pay the bills for a few months and hopefully lead to more clients.

She pulled the contract out of the folder she had brought in and handed it to Margie. "If you want to take a day to look it over, you're welcome to."

Margie scoffed and waved her hand in a dismissive gesture. "I don't need that. You were practically family, and I know you are an honest woman. Just give me a second to read over it."

Kaitlyn tensed at the words. Practically family. She had once hoped they would be family as marrying Dillon had been part of her dreams. But he had other plans. She had been hoping he would stay close and they would continue to date through college, but he'd left stating his need to see the world. However, that was the past. She needed to focus on the present. And that present was Margie who needed a moment alone. "Of course. Would you like some water or hot tea?"

"Tea would be wonderful, thank you."

Kaitlyn pushed back her chair and quietly exited the room, pulling the door shut behind her.

"Well?" Melody's voice caught her off guard and Kaitlyn jumped and threw her hand over her heart. How did she approach so quietly?

"Melody, you scared me. Don't sneak up on people like that."

"Sorry, I'm just really excited to know how it went."

Kaitlyn put her finger to her lips and motioned Melody to follow her to the kitchen. "She's looking over the contract right now, but she loved the third design."

Melody clapped her hands together and bounced on her toes. Even though she was in her late twenties, Melody looked like a young girl when she got excited. "Ooh, I knew she would. It was my favorite too. So, when do we start?"

"In two days. Do you think you can get the phones forwarded so we can still get calls when we're both working there?" Kaitlyn opened one of the cabinets and took out a mug and a tea bag, then she filled the mug with hot water from their cooler and dropped the bag in.

"Of course." Melody's face clouded in confusion. "Where exactly is this lodge?"

"Keystone, so about ninety minutes with no traffic. However, this time of year, I'd bet on two to three hours to be safe, so I just plan on staying." Kaitlyn laughed at Melody's wide eyes and shocked expression. "You don't have to stay. If you can come down a few times a week, we should still finish in time. I'll hire a crew that can stay at the lodge."

"Okay, that I can do. I just can't leave Trixie alone all day every day. She's finally stopped tearing up everything in sight, but I'm afraid boarding her for three weeks would send her into a relapse." Trixie was the yellow lab puppy that Melody had picked up a few weeks after breaking up with her boyfriend. She claimed it was because she was lonely, but Kaitlyn thought it had more to do with her biological clock ticking. A puppy wasn't exactly a baby, but the care involved was pretty close.

"You should have crate trained her," Kaitlyn said with a shake of her head.

"I know, but she had the saddest face when I put her in there. These big droopy eyes and I swear her mouth turned into a frown. It was more than I could take."

Kaitlyn chuckled. Melody was not only an animal fan, but also a bit of an exaggerator. "You are such a softie."

"I know. Hey, wait, what are you going to do with Jack?"

"I'm going to take him with me. I figured he could use a vacation as well, and I always loved winter at the lodge. I put the clause in the contract, and speaking of the contract, I better get back in there. Wish me luck."

"I will, but you don't need it. You're a natural at this, Kaitlyn."

Kaitlyn smiled and walked cautiously back to the conference room. The mug was warm in her hands, but she was careful not to spill it. The last thing she needed was a stain on her shirt or a burn on her hand before a big job.

Margie was scanning the last page as she entered. She glanced up and smiled. "Everything appears to be in order."

"Oh, I'm so glad." Kaitlyn set the tea cup down in front of Margie and held out a pen.

"It's just too bad you and Dillon never got together," Margie continued as she picked up the pen and signed. "Having a decorator in the family would be such a benefit."

Dillon's name again. Was Margie going to drop it in every conversation? Didn't she know that Kaitlyn had adored Dillon, but his love must not have been as deep? Kaitlyn's cheeks began to ache from the pasted smile, but she nodded.

"I guess we'll just have to hire you for all our jobs. IF you do amazing this time that is." She laid the pen down and picked up the cup. Though she smiled, Kaitlyn wasn't sure if the smile was genuine or a carefully veiled threat. Suddenly she wondered what she had gotten herself into.

DILLON STARED at the email from his mother. The lodge back home had been picked to be in The Travel Magazine Winter Edition and his mother was throwing a huge release party for the occasion. He had just been thinking about how much he missed the snow, and Keystone would definitely have some this time of year. He could take a few weeks off and relax there. Do some skiing and maybe take some pictures to get inspired again. He hadn't booked a job in a few weeks, and he knew it was because he wasn't inspired.

Plus, he held fond memories of Christmas at the lodge. His mother always decorated to the nines, and she made cookies and bought gifts for all the children who stayed there during the holidays. There were coloring contests and popcorn stringing. And on Christmas Day, his father would dress up as Santa in the morning to hand out the gifts.

He glanced over at Shana who sat at the vanity she had insisted he buy for his rental house even though they didn't live together. She was brushing her long blond hair and carefully counting each stroke. He didn't understand it, but she swore that brushing her hair one hundred times a day made it strong and shiny. "Hey, Shana, what do you think of going to a ski lodge for a few weeks?"

"I don't think so."

"Why not? You don't have any jobs over Christmas do you?" Shana was a model for a swimwear company. She generally stayed busy, but the holidays were much slower.

"I don't do rustic lodges in the mountains." She ran the brush through her long blond hair again. "Fifty three." Her gaze never left the mirror. "I don't like being cold, remember?"

Dillon rolled his eyes. Shana was fun in a lot of areas, but she refused to do anything where she might get cold. Pools had to be near hot tub temperature. Beaches were fine, but she rarely went in the water. Skiing was out of the question as was sledding, building a snowman, or ice skating. It was times like this that he wondered why they were still together. It was no wonder he hadn't been able to pick a ring for her. They were opposites in nearly every way except for their love of photography. Of course while he loved taking pictures, she loved having pictures taken of her, but it had kept them going for six months now.

"It's my family's lodge, Shana. They're having a big party, and I thought it would be a good chance for you to meet my mom." Plus it would give him a chance to get his mother's opinion about Shana. If his mother liked Shana, then he would know his insecurities were just that, but if she didn't, it would solidify his misgivings about this relationship before he made a massive mistake.

The brush paused and her shoulders rose slightly with her inhaled breath. "I'm not sure I'm ready to do family yet either, Dillon."

Dillon ran a hand through his short dark hair. "What are we doing then, Shana?"

She shrugged. "Having fun. I'm just not ready for any strings, Dillon."

Right. Strings. Boy was he glad he hadn't bought a ring now. He wasn't asking her to marry him, just meet his mother, but just like the cold, Shana wasn't a fan of anything that felt too personal. Dillon could only imagine how she would have reacted if he had proposed. "Well, I'm going anyway. I haven't seen my mother in ages, and Christmas is always huge at the lodge."

She put the brush down and turned to face him. "You're going to be gone over Christmas?"

"I am. I don't have a pressing job, and I miss my mother. That's why I wanted you to come with me, but maybe instead of a holiday together what we need is a holiday apart."

Shana sighed. "I don't want to break up, Dillon. I just want to go somewhere tropical." Of course she did. She wanted him to take her on another tropical vacation like he had a few months ago. The problem was, he didn't really have the money to keep flying her off to exotic places. His job earned him decent money, but it had been dwindling quickly since meeting Shana. He couldn't believe he had been thinking of purchasing a ring. It wasn't time to propose. It was time to cut his losses.

He stood and crossed to her. "I know. It's me breaking it off. I've been trying to figure out where we should go from here for quite some time, and this solidifies it for me. I want someone adventurous. Someone who is willing to go places with me and meet my family." Someone like Kaitlyn he thought to himself. Kaitlyn? He hadn't thought of her in a while. Why was she popping into his head now? "It's been fun, Shana, but I'm looking for more."

Her blue eyes turned to ice and narrowed to slits as she regarded him. Then she shrugged and flicked her long hair over her shoulder. "Whatever. It's your loss, Dillon. I'll have no trouble finding someone else."

Dillon knew that was true. Though he was a good looking guy, Shana was a bombshell with her perfect figure, long blond hair, and blue eyes. He had constantly had to deal with guys hitting on her in front of him the last six months, and he could only imagine how many hit on her when he wasn't around.

"I'm sure you won't, but we just want different things right now. I think this is for the best."

She rolled her eyes one more time, grabbed her brush from the vanity, tucked it in her purse, and walked out of his rented house.

Dillon sighed as the front door shut. He hadn't planned to spend the holidays alone, but it would be better than spending it with a woman he didn't really love. The question was... would he ever find a woman he loved? Dillon thought back over his last few relationships. He had ended all of them. Shana was too obsessed with money. Natalie was too athletic. Kara was too quiet. As he replayed the relationships in his head, he realized he had compared every one of them to Kaitlyn.

Kaitlyn, his girlfriend from ten years ago, who even though she had been the same age as him, she had always seemed a little younger, especially after her mother died. He'd taken her under his wing, and they'd become best friends and then dated. They'd spent tons of time at the lodge cuddling in front of the fire and they'd gone to prom together. At one point, he'd even thought they would get married, but then graduation had come. She'd wanted to stay close to home and attend design school while he'd wanted to see the world. He'd always thought he would come home and they would get together, but it hadn't happened and he'd forgotten her as time moved on. At least he thought he'd forgotten her. What if he'd been comparing every woman to Kaitlyn Bell because she had stolen his heart at the age of seventeen, and he'd never really gotten it back?

CHAPTER 3

"W here are we going again, Mom?" Jack asked as he entered the living room with his little suitcase rolling behind him.

"To a lodge I used to hang out at a lot," Kaitlyn said as she gathered the items she had purchased the day before. "Now, I'll have to be working a lot of the time, but there will still be plenty for you to do. However, you should still bring your tablet. Do you have it?"

He nodded and pulled the tablet and charger out of his bag. "I brought my bear too, Mom, and all the clothes you told me to."

"Good job." She ruffled his hair and ran through her mental list one more time. Kaitlyn had purchased the paint supplies and wallpaper. Melody would be picking up the new furniture and bringing it tomorrow. "Okay, I think we're ready. Let's load up."

She locked the door behind them and put the bags in the back of her SUV as Jack climbed up in his carseat and buckled in. Before she started the car, Kaitlyn took a deep breath and sent a prayer up for peace and the ability to do this job without getting stuck in past memories.

KAITLYN PULLED into the lot of the lodge and parked the car. "We're here, Jack," she said as she turned off the engine. He looked up from his tablet and nodded. The drive had been quiet as he had been engrossed in a game the whole time. On one hand, it had been nice as she didn't have to answer his constant questions, but it had also given her lots of time to think and reminisce.

She opened the back of the SUV and grabbed the few items she could. She would have to make another few trips, but at least she could get started with these. Jack stood by his car door waiting for her.

"Walk carefully, Jack. The snow can be deceiving if there is ice underneath." The walkway was covered with snow from the night before. Kaitlyn stepped carefully to avoid slipping and kept an eye on Jack. She didn't want to damage her goods or either one of them. This job was too important. Thankfully, it appeared the groundskeeper had laid down salt, as neither the ground nor the porch was very slippery. However, she was forced to juggle her bags when she reached the door.

"Here, let me help you with that."

Kaitlyn glanced over to see a handsome man striding her direction from the side of the porch. His uniform suggested that perhaps he was the groundskeeper or at least part of the crew.

"Thank you. I suppose I should have remembered I would need a hand to open the door."

He smiled at her and pulled the door open. "It happens all the time."

Kaitlyn chuckled and dropped her eyes. She supposed that was true. Vacationers always seemed to bring too many bags. She knew she did. Of course, she hadn't been on a vacation in months. Maybe they could afford one after this job. Before she could reply to the man though, Margie's voice filled the room.

"Ah, Kaitlyn darling, are we ready to begin then?" Margie stepped from behind the desk wearing a bright red suit and a string of pearls.

Kaitlyn smiled as she set down her items. It appeared Margie hadn't changed much in the time Kaitlyn had been away. Her Christmas outfits were always delightful and entertaining. Kaitlyn had once asked Dillon how many she had, and he claimed she owned thirty two. One for every day in December and a spare in case one got dirty. They had tried to sneak into her closet once so he could prove it, but she had caught them and given them a tongue lashing. Evidently her closet was where she kept Christmas gifts until they were wrapped as well, and she hated when recipients ruined their surprise.

"Well, almost. I have a few more bags in the car, and I'm waiting for the crew."

Margie's eyes flicked to the man behind Kaitlyn. "Julian, will you be a dear and get the rest of the items Kaitlyn needs?"

"Oh, no, that's okay. I can get them myself," Kaitlyn said hurriedly.

"Nonsense, dear, it is part of Julian's job description."

Kaitlyn looked to the sandy haired man. A reddish blond beard covered the bottom of his face, but it was his penetrating gaze that unnerved her. He shrugged and flashed a charming smile. "It is part of my job. Tell me what you drive, and I'll be happy to get what you need."

"Okay," Kaitlyn said. She held out her keys. "It's the blue Honda CRV out front. The bags I need are in the back."

He took the keys and stepped back out the front door.

"You must be Jack," Margie said turning her attention to Kaitlyn's son.

He nodded.

"Well, it's nice to meet you, Jack. While we wait for Julian, shall I show you to your room? I'm afraid I only had two available, so I hope your crew doesn't mind sharing."

"I'm sure it will be fine. The crew is two brothers, so they're probably used to sharing." Kaitlyn grabbed her personal items, nudged Jack to walk ahead of her, and followed Margie up the stairs and down the hallway. She stifled a sigh when Margie opened up the sunshine room. Kaitlyn hadn't been at the lodge in ages, not since her senior year, but she had spent the last few days looking over the layout and knew where each room was. The Sunshine room was her least favorite room. She had never been a fan of yellow walls or the false cheeriness they tried to instill.

As Margie opened the door, Kaitlyn tried to keep her face stoic. The room was worse than she remembered. The bright yellow wallpaper was cracked and peeling eliciting a creepy feeling and the faded flowered bedspread oozed depression.

"We're staying here?" Jack's little face scrunched in confusion, and Kaitlyn shot him a warning look to be quiet, complete with gritted teeth behind a tight smile.

"Oh, I'm sorry about this. Perhaps I should have you redo this room when you are done with the living room," Margie said as she glanced around the room.

"It will be fine, Margie. I'm here for work remember? And Jack will be fine, but I would be happy to redo this room. I've never been a fan of yellow."

"Yes, I'm not sure what I was thinking either," Margie said with a laugh.

Kaitlyn set her bag down on the bed and motioned for

Jack to do the same. They then followed Margie back to the main room. "Okay, so the first thing we need to do is move the furniture out of the room."

"Maybe we can help with that."

Kaitlyn turned toward the front door and smiled. The men she had hired had arrived. Ryan, her carpenter, and his brother, Richard. These two were not only great handymen but added muscle. "Ryan, Richard, I'd like you to meet Margie Fields, the owner."

"Pleased to make your acquaintance, ma'am," Ryan said as he took off his cowboy hat and issued a little bow. Richard said nothing but repeated the gesture.

"Now that accent doesn't sound Coloradoan to me," Margie said as she appraised the two men.

"No, ma'am. We're from Montana originally. We came out here to visit a cousin once and liked it so much we decided to move."

"Ah, that would explain it then. Well, welcome to Fields Lodge."

"Margie, is there some where we can put the furniture until I can get a truck here to haul it away?" Kaitlyn asked. Melody would be coming up in the morning with the new pieces.

"I can show them a place outside," Julian said from the doorway. In his arms were the rest of her bags.

"Thank you. That would be lovely. You can just put those bags down in the corner."

Julian obliged and handed Kaitlyn back her keys. Then he waited until Ryan and Richard had a couch in hand and he opened the door and led them outside.

"Jack, how about you come in the kitchen with me?" Margie asked touching his shoulder. "I made a plate of chocolate chip cookies."

Jack turned eager eyes to Kaitlyn and she smiled and nodded. "Just one though. I don't want you to ruin your appetite for dinner."

When Jack and Margie filed out of the room, Kaitlyn took the opportunity to inspect the walls. They appeared to be in decent shape, but she needed to make sure they were clean and devoid of holes.

The men re-appeared and took the next couch out as Kaitlyn continued scanning the walls. About the time they finished clearing the furniture, she had finished her inspection. "The walls look good. I think we can begin painting tonight and getting the wallpaper up."

"Wonderful," Margie said clapping her hands from the kitchen entryway. "Then how about we take a break and I'll whip us up some food?"

"That sounds lovely ma'am. Richard and I would like to clean up first. Is there any way you could show us to our room first?" Ryan asked as he glanced up the stairs.

"Oh, yes, of course. Follow me."

Margie led the men upstairs, leaving Kaitlyn alone in the living room with Julian.

"Will your husband be joining the two of you as well?" he asked as Kaitlyn reviewed her mental list. Painting and wallpapering, she wanted Ryan to build a new mantle for the fireplace, pick up whatever pieces Melody hadn't been able to acquire, and of course, sew the pillows. The list was daunting, but she still believed they could be done in time.

"No, Jack's father is no longer in the picture," she said slowly.

"Oh, I'm sorry to hear that. Well, I best get back to work. Please don't hesitate to call if you need anything."

"Sure, thank you." As the man left, Kaitlyn wasn't sure if he was just being nice or if he was attracted to her.

DILLON SET his drink down and waved to his friend Grant as he entered the restaurant. Grant nodded and made his way through the crowd to where Dillon was sitting.

"What's up, man?"

"Not much. Just wanted to hang out before I leave for the holidays. You want to get a booth?" He nodded his head to a free booth in the back.

"Sure." Grant followed him to the booth and folded his long frame in. "Where you going?"

Dillon slid in to the other side and set his drink down. "Back to my parent's lodge in Keystone."

Grant's head fell forward and his brow arched. "You got Shana to go to a lodge in Colorado? This I gotta hear."

Dillon rolled his eyes and chuckled. Grant knew Shana too well. "No, Shana and I broke up. It's just me going."

A low whistle escaped Grant's mouth. "I thought you were looking at rings."

Dillon rolled his eyes. "I was. How crazy was that?"

"Well, how did she take it?"

Dillon swirled the straw in his drink. "What do you mean? She told me it was my loss and there were a dozen other men lined up for her. Probably true too. I mean you've seen her."

"Wow, what a piece of work. Why were you with this girl again?" Grant picked up the menu from the holder on the end of the table and scanned the options.

That was a good question. One Dillon had been asking himself for the last few hours. Six months of his life was just gone. Six months and a few paychecks he would never get back. "I honestly don't know. I guess I thought our love of photography would be enough to sustain a relationship."

"You mean your love of photography and her love of being photographed."

"Yes, well. Needless to say, it didn't work out."

Grant lowered the menu and stared evenly at Dillon. "You've been dating one wrong girl after the other since I met you. What exactly are you running from?"

Dillon shook his head, surprised that his friend was so

perceptive. "I think… my past. Lately, I can't get this girl out of my head. My ex-girlfriend from high school."

"Ooh, now this is good." Grant set the menu on the table and folded his hands over it, leaning forward. "Who is she and where is she now?"

"Her name was Kaitlyn Bell. I don't know if it still is. I haven't seen or heard from her since I left nearly ten years ago."

"If this girl meant so much to you then why'd you leave?"

The waitress appeared at the table and took their food order. Dillon was glad for the slight reprieve to gather his thoughts. "I don't think I knew how much she meant to me. I was young and stupid, and I didn't know what I had. She wanted to go to design school, and I wanted to see the world. However, I realized recently that every woman I've dated, I've compared to her."

"Man, you gotta find this girl and see what's going on with her now. Otherwise, you got no hope for a future relationship."

Dillon nodded. Grant was a wise man and a good friend. The only problem was… he had no idea how to even begin looking for Kaitlyn.

CHAPTER 4

"Mom, can we go exploring today?" Jack sat across from her at the kitchen table eating homemade pancakes. And not just regular pancakes. Margie had decorated the pancakes with red syrup and whip cream to make them look like Santa Claus.

Kaitlyn yawned and checked her watch. She, Ryan, and Richard had been up late painting and wallpapering, but it had had to be done in order to be dry for today. "Well, Melody is supposed to be here with the furniture." His face fell, and Kaitlyn hurried to continue. "But, let me text her and see how long she'll be. Maybe it will give us some time to hang out before she gets here."

Kaitlyn tapped out a quick message to Melody and waited for a response. A moment later, her phone buzzed.

Sorry, held up at the furniture store. It will be another

few hours.

"Well, good news, bud. Melody is running late, so we have a few hours to explore."

His eyes lit up. "Can we build a snowman?"

Kaitlyn laughed. "Sure, we can build a snowman. Finish up there and we'll get dressed for the cold."

Jack proceeded to shove the rest of the pancakes in his mouth. All Kaitlyn could do was smile and shake her head. "Dm," he said, his mouth still stuffed with food.

"Finish chewing first." Kaitlyn rolled her eyes and washed her mug out in the sink. She smiled as she set the mug, decorated like a Christmas tree, on the counter.

"All done." Jack opened his mouth to show her it was empty. "Can we go outside now?"

"Yes, baby bear, come on, let's get you layered up."

On the way to their room, Kaitlyn stopped at Ryan and Richard's room. She was pleased to see the brothers up and dressed when they opened the door. "Melody is going to be a little late. Do you think you guys could do the mantel this morning?"

"Sure," Ryan said. "We'll get started right after breakfast."

"Thank you."

Kaitlyn continued down the hall to the Sunshine Room. After adding a jacket, gloves, and a hat to Jack, she led the way outside. The snow was blindingly white, and Kaitlyn wished she had remembered a pair of sunglasses.

"There's so much snow," Jack said, the awe evident in his voice as he looked around.

"Yep. Plenty of snow to build an amazing snowman. So, let's get to it." Kaitlyn bent down and began rolling up the snow into a ball. Jack quickly joined in and the two were soon laughing and giggling as the ball of snow grew.

When the bottom layer was finished, they began rolling the second, but when it was done, Kaitlyn realized too late that it was too heavy for her to lift."

"Does that mean we can't finish?" Jack's face was a painting of disappointment.

"Maybe I can help."

Kaitlyn turned around to see Julian behind them. "Oh, we couldn't. I know for a fact *this* isn't in your job description."

He smiled and glanced back at the lodge. "No, but I know Mrs. Fields would have my hide if I could have helped and sent a young boy back inside without a snowman."

"Please, Mom? He can help us real quick and then get back to work."

"Fine." Kaitlyn held up her hands. "I am clearly outnumbered."

"I'm glad you came around." Julian squatted down on one side of the ball of snow and Kaitlyn took the other. Between the two of them, they were able to heft the heavy ball onto the low body.

Jack raised his fist in triumph. "Yes, just one more to go."

"My advice is don't make the head too large or you'll have the same problem." Julian flashed her a wink before disappearing around the side of the lodge.

Okay, so a wink usually meant interest. The question was... was she interested back?

"Come on, Mom. Let's finish the head."

Kaitlyn dragged her eyes back to her son and smiled. "Right, the head. How could I forget?" They rolled up a smaller ball of snow, and this time Kaitlyn was able to muscle it up herself. The snowman was eye level with her when they finished.

"Okay, kiddo, I'm getting cold. You ready to head in?"

"Yeah, I guess. Can we come back out again later? Maybe give him a scarf and a hat?"

She smiled down at him and grabbed one of his gloved hands. "Sure, we can probably do that."

They headed back into the lodge, and after taking off their boots, coats, gloves, and hats, they wandered into the kitchen.

"Did you two have fun out there?" Margie asked as they entered. She sat at the kitchen table with a piece of paper and a pen. Her sweater was red and fuzzy.

"Yeah, it was fun. I want to go out again."

"Well, perhaps your mother will let you come with me

later. I'm filling out a grocery list and need to run into town."

Jack nodded and turned to Kaitlyn. "Can I Mom?"

Kaitlyn smiled at Margie. Whether the woman was just being nice to Jack or whether she was thinking of Kaitlyn and the work ahead of her this afternoon, Kaitlyn was grateful. "Of course you can. Do you have any hot chocolate, Margie? I sure could use a little warm-me-up."

"Certainly, dear. In the cupboard above the stove."

"Can I have some too?" Jack asked. "With marshmallows?"

Kaitlyn chuckled as she opened the cupboard. Jack loved marshmallows. He was always bugging her to buy them in the store, and more than once she caught him sneaking into the bag. S'mores were his favorite treat, and if she let him pick the cereal, it usually had marshmallows in it. "You're in luck. It seems there is a package up here with little marshmallows."

She took the two packets down along with two mugs and set the kettle to boiling on the stove. When it whistled a few minutes later, she filled the mugs and brought them back to the table. Jack thanked her and cupped his small hands around the mug, blowing on the steam as it rose to send it spiraling away.

Kaitlyn smiled as she sipped her own mug. She hated that Jack had no father figure in his life, but she was so glad she had gotten him away from her abusive ex-husband before he could be scarred by it. Perhaps one day God would send her the right man and Jack could have a second chance at a father.

I T WAS late in the afternoon when Melody arrived. She entered the lodge looking frazzled and stressed.

"What took so long?" Kaitlyn asked.

"The traffic was horrendous. Did I mention I don't like traffic? And I like it even less in a big U-Haul truck." Melody had grown up in a small town in Texas and though Denver was no small town, she had developed a routine of driving to work, stores, and the park. Kaitlyn knew she avoided the interstate at all costs.

"Well, thank you for coming. It was well timed. As you can see, we cleared out the room yesterday and got the wall-paper hung and the other walls painted last night. Ryan finished the mantel about an hour ago. Once we get the furniture in that you have, I'll just need to find whatever pieces are missing and decorate."

"Did I hear someone say they needed furniture unloaded?" Ryan asked entering the room.

"Yes. Melody has arrived with the U-Haul."

"Great. I'll go get Richard, and we can get started."

"I'd be happy to help too," Julian said. Kaitlyn hadn't even heard the door open, but there he stood in the doorway.

"Who's the hunk?" Melody whispered as she leaned closer to Kaitlyn. As Melody had worked with Ryan and Richard before, Kaitlyn assumed she was talking about Julian.

"Thanks, Julian," Kaitlyn said. "This is my friend, Melody."

"Pleased to meet you," he said with a nod.

"You as well." Melody's words sounded breathless, and her eyes never left Julian's. Kaitlyn rolled her eyes. Melody was like a window shopper of men. She bounced from one to another like a socialite following the latest trend.

Thankfully, Richard and Ryan returned then and the group headed outside to the truck. Melody handed over the key, and Ryan unlocked the back and rolled up the door. The U-Haul was stacked with couches, lamps, tables, paintings. Kaitlyn even saw a few pillows.

"Did you get everything?" she asked Melody. "That's a full truck."

"Almost," Melody said with a smile. "You did a great job securing everything. All I had to do was pick it up."

"Well, let's get started unloading it," Ryan said as he pulled out the ramp and then climbed into the back of the truck. They started with the little pieces that were closest to the back. Even Kaitlyn and Melody were able to help with the lamps and pillows. Soon, they hit the heavier items, and the girls stayed in the living room and designated where each piece should go.

Melody had found two perfect couches which Kaitlyn arranged to face the fireplace. They had the perfect view of the new mantel Ryan had constructed. A repurposed wood coffee table fit nicely in between them.

"That's all the furniture, Kaitlyn," Ryan said. "Is there anything else you need Richard and I for?"

"No, it seems all we have left to do is hang pictures and decorate for Christmas. Thank you again for your help on such short notice." She held out her hand, and Ryan shook it.

"Always a pleasure to do business with you, Kaitlyn."

"That goes for me as well," Richard said, shaking her hand before following Ryan out of the lodge.

Kaitlyn surveyed the room. With the furniture neatly arranged, she could now see where the pictures needed to go.

"Is there anything I can do to help?" Julian asked.

Kaitlyn jumped when she realized he was just behind her. "Yes, can you get a hammer and nails, so Melody and I can get the pictures hung?"

"It would be my pleasure," he said before throwing her a wink and exiting the room.

"I think someone likes you," Melody teased as the door closed behind him.

Heat flared across Kaitlyn's face. "I'm sure he's just being nice."

"Uh huh. Well, I wish he'd be that nice my direction. I mean it's not like you date."

"I date," Kaitlyn said.

"When was your last one?" Melody asked, hands on her hips.

"It was…." Kaitlyn thought but she couldn't remember her last date. "Never mind. My love life isn't up for discussion. We need to finish this room, so I can begin decorating."

Julian reappeared a few minutes later with a hammer and some nails. He patiently waited while Kaitlyn decided which picture needed to go where and then hammered in the nail and secured the picture.

"Well, this looks wonderful," Margie said as she entered the room with Jack right behind her. Kaitlyn and Melody had just finished hanging the last picture. "I was coming to check on progress, but it appears you will definitely be done in time for the photographer."

Kaitlyn surveyed the room once more. Everything had come into place nicely. The walls had been spotless, so hanging the wallpaper and repainting had occurred quickly. The mantel for the fireplace drew the eye's attention, and all of the pieces Melody had brought fit her vision to a tee. It looked cover worthy, and the only thing left to do was decorate it for Christmas. "Yes, Margie, I believe we will."

"Wonderful, well I'm going to take some guests down to town. They want to know the best places to shop, and since I need to get groceries, I figured this would be a good outing for everyone. I'll keep Jack with me. We'll be back later." She turned to Julian. "Can you get a van ready to drive us?"

"Of course, Mrs. Fields," he said before ducking out the front door.

Melody glanced at her watch. "I should get going too. I need to get back to Trixie before she tears the place up."

"Do you think you can come back tomorrow? We can probably finish in a few hours."

"Sure thing."

As everyone left, Kaitlyn wandered into the kitchen to make a cup of tea and have a light snack. Margie said they were low on food, but she had made a batch of Christmas cookies earlier in the day. Kaitlyn had been too busy to have one earlier, but she was pleased to see one lone cookie still sitting on the plate.

As she sipped her tea and nibbled her cookie, she thought about how she wanted the room to look. With the rustic decor, gold would look exceptionally good in the room, but then she couldn't put icicles on the tree. Unless they made gold ones. She'd have to check the town out herself if she didn't find any.

She finished the cookie and tea and washed the cup out in the sink. Time to get decorating. Kaitlyn knew Margie had a ton of Christmas decorations around somewhere, but unfortunately she was in town shopping. Kaitlyn pursed her lips. There had to be an attic or a basement somewhere but she couldn't remember ever seeing it. Then she remembered the old sunroom. The guests rarely used it, but she and Dillon often had. It was a perfect room for them to kick off their muddy or snow-covered boots before entering the rest of the lodge.

And if Kaitlyn remembered correctly, there was a shelving unit full of boxes in that room. In fact, other than a shelf for their shoes and a small table, the shelving unit had been the only other thing in the room. Kaitlyn had often wondered what was in those rows of boxes, and now seemed the perfect time to find out.

The room was at the back of the lodge, and the outside sun spilled in through the large windows as Kaitlyn entered. Sure enough, the room was exactly as she had pictured it. Rows and rows of boxes still lined the shelf across the far wall of the room. Kaitlyn sighed. She had no idea where to start, and none of the boxes were labeled. How in the world did Margie know what was in them? Perhaps the better question was *did* Margie know what was in them?

She pulled the closest box out and opened the lid. Neatly folded towels sat on top. Kaitlyn placed the box on the floor and gently dug underneath the towels, but that appeared to be all that was in the box. She folded the top back down and replaced it on the shelf. One down and only about twenty more to go.

DILLON PULLED into the lot of the lodge and looked around in surprise. Where were all the cars? This was normally the busy time of year for the lodge. From mid November to New Year's, but there were few cars in the parking lot.

He parked the truck and grabbed his bags from the back. The snow crunched under his feet as he walked to the entrance. The front door was unlocked as usual. Though near Keystone, the lodge was far enough from the main town that people didn't usually stumble upon it without knowing where it was, so they left the door unlocked.

"Hello," Dillon called as he pushed open the door and stepped into the foyer. The foyer held a small waiting area and a front desk that an employee generally manned, but today the desk was empty.

"Hello?" He stepped through the archway into the living room. His eyes widened as he took in the decor. His mother must have hired someone to update the room as he could still smell the faint odor of fresh paint, and he certainly didn't remember some of the pieces of furniture. Now, if only she would let someone redo the guest rooms and kitchen as well. While he knew his mother kept busy, he also knew she could get more customers and raise her rates if she updated the lodge.

And speaking of his mother, where was she? His father had passed away a few years ago, but his mother was usually flitting around the lodge making small talk and cups of tea, but today there was no sound. He wandered into the kitchen, but it too was empty. Curious, but his bags were getting heavy. He could investigate after he dropped them off, so he made his way back to the front desk and opened the log book to see what was available. His mother used to keep one of the rooms open for him, but when he had stopped coming home every Christmas, she had informed him he would have to reserve one like every other guest. He just hoped she had an empty one.

He scanned the entries, glad to see one room open. It wasn't his favorite room, but at least it wasn't The Sunshine Room. He'd always hated the colors of that one. After jotting his name down, so his mother wouldn't fill the room, he headed up the stairs.

The Forest Room was at the far left end of the hall. Dillon pushed open the door and sighed as the solid green walls attacked him. Why his mother had ever insisted on giving each room a color theme was beyond him. However, the bed was made and the room would do while he was here. He hoisted his bags on the bed but decided he would unpack them later. His stomach rumbled as he made his way back to the kitchen, and he opened the fridge to see what goodies his mother had stored.

Surprise colored his face as the mostly bare fridge stared back at him. Maybe his mother was shopping in town. She definitely couldn't feed guests with what was in here. A few condiments, some meat and cheese, and a loaf of bread. Dillon had been hoping for more, but a sandwich would have to do for now. Perhaps he could beg her to cook a big dinner tonight.

He took two slices from the bread bag and placed them on a paper towel. Then he opened the drawer where the silverware was kept. His fingers had just grasped the knife when he heard a loud thud. Quickly, he bypassed the butter knife and grabbed a sharper knife, clutching it tightly.

With quiet footsteps, he made his way out of the kitchen and toward the back of the house where the sound had come from. Guests rarely went back there as it was more of the family living part of the house.

"Darn it." The female voice was followed by another crash and Dillon burst into the sun room.

"Don't move." He held the knife up in a threatening position hoping he wouldn't have to actually use it.

The woman screamed, dropped the box in her arms, and turned around.

A vice grip squeezed Dillon's lungs, and the hand holding the knife lowered to his side. "Kaitlyn?"

"Dillon?" Shock threaded her voice and he knew the confused expression on her face must mirror his own.

Kaitlyn Bell back in front of him. Was this fate? "What are you doing here?" He kicked himself mentally. That wasn't what he wanted to say. Why were words failing him now?

"I could ask you the same question." Her hands curled into fists and jammed onto her slim hips. Dillon smiled at the way her chin tilted up and to the right when she was angry. "Your mother said you wouldn't be here."

That was odd considering his mother had sent him an email about the party in a few days, but he decided to play dumb until he knew what was going on. "I hadn't planned to, but my schedule opened up."

She shook her head, sending her dark locks swirling about her head. "Well, this isn't going to work. I took this job because your mother assured me you would be gone." Her eyes were fierce, not the warm chocolate depths he remembered from high school.

Dillon set the knife on the fireplace mantle and stepped toward her. "What job?"

Kaitlyn leaned down and began picking up the doilies and tablecloths that had spilled from the box. "Your mother hired me to redecorate the living room of the lodge. I'm almost done here, but the photographer will be here in a few days. I don't need a distraction."

She considered him a distraction? Did that mean she still had feelings for him as well? Dillon dropped to the floor and helped her gather the loose items. "Mother didn't know I was coming. I didn't tell her, but I'll stay out of your way. You won't even know I'm here." That was not what he wanted at all, but it appeared Kaitlyn still harbored hard feelings from their last encounter.

"Thank you," she said as she took the items from him, but her voice was still cold, controlled. She stood up and her eyes raked over him. "I don't know, Dillon. I have a hard time believing you'll stay out of sight."

He traced the pattern of an x across his chest and flashed his most charming smile at her. "Cross my heart."

She let out a enormous sigh and rolled her eyes. "Fine. Well, as long as you're here, maybe you can help me."

Dillon issued a small bow. "It would be my pleasure, mademoiselle."

Kaitlyn shook her head and rolled her eyes. "Do you know where your mother keeps the Christmas decorations?"

"Is that what you were looking for?" He eyed the shelf. "I don't think she keeps them here."

Kaitlyn sighed. "I have no idea where else to look except her closet, but I don't feel right going in there."

"Me neither," he said with a laugh.

"Why does your mother have so many towels and table-cloths anyway? That's all I've found in every box."

Dillon shook his head. "She likes to have something for every season, I guess." His stomach rumbled reminding him he had never finished his sandwich. "Listen, I don't know when Mother will return, and there is nothing in the fridge to eat. What do you say we go grab a pizza to kill some time? You can ask her about the Christmas decorations when we get back."

Kaitlyn bit her lip and he could sense her hesitation. "It's just pizza, Kaitlyn. Nothing more, and you have to eat right?"

"Yeah, I suppose." Her words came out slowly as if every word was a challenge.

"Look, if you're afraid of being out with me, then I'll go pick one up and bring it back. How's that?" Dillon was hoping a little reverse psychology would work on her. Maybe if he acted like he didn't care, she would. He bit back a smile when it worked.

She shook her head. "No, it's fine. We can go get food. I'm hungry myself. I had a cookie earlier, but it didn't fill me up."

"You had a cookie? I didn't see any in the kitchen."

"That's because I had the last one." She flashed a smile at him. "Just let me change real quick."

"Sure." He wanted to freshen up a bit as well. "Meet you up front in fifteen?"

"All right."

They both headed down the hallway that led to the rooms and then she turned right as he turned left. He reached his door first but waited just a moment to see which room she turned into. A slight chuckle escaped his lips as he saw her duck into the Sunshine Room. Dillon knew Kaitlyn hated the color yellow.

He pushed open his own door and closed it behind him. After rifling through his bags for his toiletries and a clean sweater, he stepped into the bathroom. There wasn't quite time for a shower, but a thorough brushing of his teeth and a new application of deodorant made him feel like a new man. He splashed a little cologne on his neck and ran a brush through his hair. The brown sweater brought out the green in his eyes and accented the dimple in his left cheek that Kaitlyn used to love.

Grabbing his wallet on the way out, he headed to the living room to wait for Kaitlyn. She appeared a moment later in a mint green sweater and a pair of jeans. Her porcelain skin radiated, and his heart skipped a beat in his chest.

"Your car or mine?" he asked as he opened the door.

"Mine. I've seen you drive." She flashed a teasing smile and pushed past him to her SUV.

Dillon shook his head and pulled the door shut behind him before following her.

KAITLYN GRIPPED the steering wheel and took a deep breath while she waited for Dillon. Her heart hammered in her chest like a jackhammer breaking up concrete. Dillon Fields in the flesh and still as handsome as ever. How in the world was she going to focus on the remaining work with his sultry smile and twinkling green eyes haunting her vision?

Maybe it wouldn't be so bad. If she could focus on anything other than how good his chest looked in his sweater and how warm his arms had once been, then maybe she could get him to help her out. With his help, she would be able to finish faster and get back to her life away from him. The problem was he looked too good in that sweater. It showed off his strong chest, and his jeans hugged his body in all the right places. Her traitorous heart sped up at the very sight of him, and her brain reminded her again this wasn't a good idea. But she was hungry. And it was just food. She would have to eat sometime.

He opened the passenger door and climbed in. A whiff of Polo Sport drifted in along with the cool air from outside. A tremble raced through her body. That had been her favorite cologne on him when they were in high school. The smell alone always made her melt, but coupled with his masculine scent, it drove her crazy. This had definitely been a bad idea.

The passenger door shut and he tapped the dash. "Shall we go?"

Kaitlyn shifted to face him. "This isn't what I planned, Dillon, and I have to stay a few more days to finish the work. So, I think we should make some rules."

His brow furrowed as he buckled his seatbelt and turned to her. "Rules? Okay, what are you thinking?"

"Um," Kaitlyn hadn't actually gotten that far. "Well, for one, we keep this strictly business."

Dillon nodded. "Okay, that I can do."

"Two, we retire to our separate rooms after sundown and remain there until sunrise at least."

"That seems a little drastic and Brady Bunchesque, but okay unless my mother requests my presence. Anything else?"

"I'm not sure, but I reserve the right to add more."

"Whatever you say." He shook his head, but the corners of his lips pulled up in a smile.

Kaitlyn hated that he thought she was kidding. This was the only way she knew to keep herself from falling for him all over again. With a shake of her head, she started the SUV. The sooner they got to the restaurant, the sooner she could get a reprieve from the intoxicating scent and the masculinity drifting her way.

Fifteen minutes later, they were seated at a booth in Gitano's Pizza place waiting for their food. But the reprieve Kaitlyn had hoped for was nowhere to be found. Yes, the scent was a little less and what lingered was masked with the smell of cheese and pizza sauce, but now she had to battle the memories as well. Gitano's had often been their Friday night date destination after the football games or before if they were late ones.

Everywhere she looked, images of the past surfaced. In the booth across from them was where he had shown her his Senior ring.

"So, Kaitlyn, I got something a few days ago."

"Oh, really?" She batted her eyes as she looked up at him. Kaitlyn knew he had received his Senior ring a few days ago, and today she was hoping he would ask her to go steady and give it to her.

"Yeah. I know we've been dating for a few months, but I can't imagine wanting to date anyone else." He pulled some-thing out of his pocket. "I wanted to know if you would be

my girlfriend and wear my ring?" Dillon held out a small gold chain that held an enormous class ring. The blue stone filled most of the middle surface and there was a football on one side and a baseball on the other.

"I'd love to." She ducked her head and he put the necklace over her hair. It fell against her chest, a heavy symbol of their love.

And across the room was the party section where they had met with a group of friends before prom Senior year.

Kaitlyn smoothed the sea foam satin of her dress and looked around the room. Who had suggested dinner at a pizza restaurant before prom? Not only was she worried about dinner causing her to puff up and be bloated, but she didn't want to spill anything on her dress. It was a rental that she had paid nearly one hundred dollars to rent for the night. She couldn't afford to spill anything on it, especially not something like pizza sauce that might never come out.

"Dillon, are you sure this is a good place to eat before dancing?"

"I don't know," he said with a laugh, "but we're here, so we might as well."

She was not convinced, but she followed him into the party room where several of their friends were already waiting.

"Penny for your thoughts," Dillon said from across the table.

Kaitlyn shook her head to clear the past and focused on

the man in front of her. Time had only made him more hand-some. His features a little more chiseled. "You couldn't afford my thoughts," she said before dropping her eyes to her drink. In reality, she didn't want to share. She didn't want him walking down memory lane with her.

"Maybe not." He paused as if unsure what to say next. Then a smile lit his face and he leaned across the tabletop as if sharing a secret. "Hey, do you remember when we ate here before prom? Whose dumb idea was that?"

"I don't know," Kaitlyn said in a tone much harsher than she meant, "but let's not talk about the past." She looked down at her watch. When was the pizza going to arrive? She could almost feel her heart stretching tendrils out and attaching once again to Dillon, but she wasn't sure she could survive another heartbreak. Plus, there was Jack to think about now. Kaitlyn couldn't date any man she couldn't see being in Jack's life.

"Okay." He stretched the syllables of the word out as if he was unsure why the topic was off limits and leaned back. "So, let's talk about the present. What have you been up to?"

"Just opening my design business. It is what I went to college for."

"Kaitlyn, I-"

She cut him off, knowing the next words out of his mouth were going to be some kind of apology, but she didn't want to hear them. Not now anyway. What could he apologize for? For wanting to see the world after high school? For never coming back? For breaking her heart and sending her running into the arms of a man she should have known to stay away from? "You know what? I'm just going to check and see what's taking our pizza so long?"

Before he could answer, she scooted out of the booth and approached the counter. At least the distance would give her a moment to compose herself. She felt as if she were on a roller coaster. One minute she was at the top enjoying the view and the next she was barreling down into the painful past where Dillon walked away from her to go see the world.

"Can I help you?" The bored voice of the male employee manning the counter grabbed her attention.

"Just checking on order number twelve. Any idea how much longer?" She smiled sweetly at the teen who would obviously rather be somewhere else.

He sighed but turned and checked the silver wheel holding the orders. "Looks like it's in the oven," he said to her. "So, another few minutes."

"Thank you," Kaitlyn said. She tapped the counter as she thought of how else to pass the time. Bathroom. She could hide out for a bit in the bathroom. Kaitlyn turned back toward Dillon and smiled. "It will just be another few minutes. I'm just going to wash my hands." She hurried into the bathroom and leaned against the closed door. How on earth was she going to get through this night? And the next three days?

She pushed away from the door and walked to the

mirror. Her wide eyes stared back at her. "You can do this, Kaitlyn. It's just dinner with an old friend. Just think of it like that. You're just friends." After another few deep breaths, she squared her shoulders and returned to the booth, please to see the pizza had arrived. She slid into her seat. "Oh good, the pizza is here."

"Yeah it looks like you wasted just enough time so that we didn't have to converse anymore," Dillon said with a wink as he placed a slice of Canadian bacon and pineapple pizza on his plate. Kaitlyn had never understood how he ate fruit on pizza. Her own half held pepperonis and cashews.

"I wasn't-" Kaitlyn began but he had caught her. There was no point denying it. " I'm sorry." She sighed and dropped her face to hide the red flush she felt. "I just don't know how to talk to you anymore. It's been so long."

"Then let's not talk. Let's just eat."

Kaitlyn smiled gratefully and picked up her own slice.

The rest of dinner passed without incident until the check arrived. The server only brought one and she and Dillon looked at each other.

"I could ask them to separate it," Kaitlyn offered.

"No, I ruined your work trip. This can be my treat."

She wanted to object more but the stubborn glint had appeared in Dillon's eye, and she knew further arguing would be pointless. Besides, she just wanted to get back to the lodge and hole up in her room where she could process the day.

"All right. This time."

Dillon whipped out his wallet and a few minutes later they exited the warm building into the cold snowy air.

"Brrr." Kaitlyn wrapped her arms around her wishing she had grabbed her coat instead. The temperature had dropped quite a few degrees when the sun went down. Luckily, her car heated up quickly and the drive back was short.

"Wow, the snow is really coming down," Dillon said beside her. "Are you sure you're okay to drive?"

She turned to him with raised eyebrows. "Um, who's the one who stayed in Colorado? I think I can drive in the snow better than you, mister Jetsetter."

He held his hands up in a display of retreat. "I was just offering. I remember how you drove in high school."

"Shut up." She punched his shoulder and he grimaced and rubbed it.

"Wow. I don't remember you hitting so hard. You been taking self defense or something?" He was kidding. It was written all over his face, but his words hit Kaitlyn and stole the playful moment.

He had no idea what had happened to her. She had never told him. But why would she? Dillon had been out of her life for years when… No, she wouldn't go down that path again. It was in the past. And it had made her stronger.

"Let's just go."

Dillon's smile faltered, and she could read the confusion in his eyes. But he shrugged and followed her to the car.

The ride back to the lodge was quiet. Kaitlyn gripped the steering wheel tightly partly because of the emotions rattling inside her and partly because of the weather. Though she had put on a brave face, she didn't enjoy driving in the snow. The white flakes were beautiful when she could sit and watch them fall, but they were very distracting when driving.

Relief flooded her when they arrived unharmed in the lodge's parking lot once more. She turned off the engine and opened the driver's side door.

"Kaitlyn, wait," Dillon said from the passenger seat.

She glanced at him, but shook her head. "Can't. See? The sun has set. It's time to be in our separate rooms. Need to get some sleep. I have a long day tomorrow." Before he could say anything else, she jetted out of the car and into the lodge.

"Oh, hello, Kaitlyn."

Kaitlyn heard Margie's voice, but she didn't stop until she was safely in her room and the door was shut behind her.

"Hey Mom," Jack said, looking up from his tablet at her. "We had so much fun. Did you know they have an ice rink?"

Kaitlyn sat on the bed and forced a smile on her face as she breathed deeply to calm her heart rate. She was going to have to find a way to distance herself from the memories of the past or she would never be able to get this job done. *Lord, please help me get through the next few weeks.* "No, that's great, honey. I'm glad you had fun."

❄

DILLON SIGHED as he exited Kaitlyn's car. His breath sent plumes of condensation into the air which curled into smoke like tendrils before disappearing into the swirling snow. He opened the door to the lodge, his shoulders low as if weighted by an invisible force.

"Dillon?"

He looked up to see his mother staring at him. "Hi, Mom."

"I suppose that explains Kaitlyn's reaction, then." His mother looked toward the stairs where undoubtedly Kaitlyn had gone, retreating to her room.

"Why did you tell her I wouldn't be here and then send me an invitation to your party?"

His mother raised a brow at him. "Well, for one thing, I didn't know you would be here. I've invited you many times to gatherings, and you never show up."

Dillon ducked his head. He had been too busy to come home as often as he should. However, now that his business wasn't doing nearly as well in Florida as it used to, he no longer had an excuse. "Okay, that's true and I'm sorry, but what's the other reason?"

"I figured if you did decide to come, it wouldn't be until the day of or the day before the event, and Kaitlyn would have been gone by then."

"Should I leave then? I mean until she's done?" Dillon

didn't want that at all. He wanted a second chance with Kaitlyn.

"Is that what you want to do?" his mother asked.

"No." He shook his head. "I've realized the last few days that I still care for her. As more than a friend. I want to date her again."

A wide smile spread across her face, and she clapped her hands. "Oh good. I was hoping you would say that. I've been praying you would wake up for years, but there's something you should know."

"What's that?"

"She has a son. Jack. He's five."

Dillon ran a hand across his chin. A son. Did that mean there was a husband? Surely not. His mother wouldn't have been so excited if there was a husband. But a kid? Dillon was sure he still had feelings for Kaitlyn, but throwing a child in the mix changed things a little. "I'm assuming there's no man in her life though."

"No, though I didn't ask what happened. Does her having a son change your mind?"

Did it? He wasn't sure. "I don't think so," he said, "but I'll need to think on it to be sure."

"Yes, of course you should." She patted his hand. "However, I think we should still discuss a plan."

Dillon chuckled at her enthusiasm, and the two retired to the kitchen to brainstorm ideas.

CHAPTER 5

Dillon woke as the sun's rays first peeked through his windows. In truth, he hadn't slept much the night before. After spending a few hours talking with his mother, thoughts of Kaitlyn and how to win her over had kept him up most of the night. Along with thoughts of her son, and how he would play into everything.

He knew he had hurt Kaitlyn when he left, but he'd had no idea how much until seeing how skittish she was around him. And how unwilling to talk about the past. He and his mother had brainstormed a few ideas, but Dillon knew he needed a grand gesture to convince her of his feelings. Words alone wouldn't convince her.

Pushing back the covers, he padded into the bathroom for a shower. The warm water pounded his back in a soothing rhythmic motion, but it did not grant him any wisdom. With a sigh, he turned the water off, toweled dry, and dressed for the day.

The lodge was quiet as he made his way to the kitchen. Everyone else was either still asleep or out already for the day. He opened the cupboards, pleased to see filters and ground coffee right where it always had been. Dillon stuck a filter in the bowl, filled it with grounds, and set the coffee brewing.

He had just poured a cup when he heard the lodge door open. "Kaitlyn?" An unfamiliar female voice called. Curious as to who this stranger was, Dillon cupped his mug and stepped into the living room.

"I don't think she's up yet. Can I help you?"

"Oh." The blond turned to him, a smile on her pretty face. She was dressed for snow with boots on, pants, at least one sweater he could see, and a scarf around her neck. In her hands was a bakery box. "And who might you be?"

"Dillon Fields," he said stepping toward her and offering his hand. He had no idea what might be in the box, but his stomach growled at the thought of food.

Her eyes widened. "Oh," she said in a very different tone.

"I guess my reputation must proceed me." He didn't know this woman but it was obvious from her reaction that Kaitlyn had filled her in. "But I'm afraid I don't know who you are."

"Oh." Again the word was uttered differently and Dillon

began to wonder if she could say anything else. "I'm Melody Phelps."

"My business partner," Kaitlyn supplied as she entered the room. Her hair was still wet, and Dillon tried not to imagine her in the shower.

"Right. Her business partner." Melody looked from Dillon to Kaitlyn and back again before clearing her throat. "Well, I hope I'm not interrupting anything, but I brought doughnuts."

"Thank heavens," Dillon said at the same time Kaitlyn uttered, "You interrupted nothing."

"Oh."

Dillon bit his lip to keep from laughing. Melody was certainly expressive given her lack of words.

"So, anyone hungry?"

Another growl escaped Dillon's stomach as she opened the box to display six different doughnuts. There was a glazed, a chocolate, one with sprinkles, a powdered dough-nut, an eclair, and his favorite - a bear claw.

"I'm starving. Mother went to the store yesterday, but she either isn't up yet or she has disappeared for the day. Either way, there's nothing cooked yet. Shall we eat in the kitchen?"

Melody looked to Kaitlyn with wide eyes as if unsure if she should accept. Kaitlyn nodded and the trio trooped into the kitchen.

"There's coffee," Dylan offered, "and cream in the fridge."

"Oh, I already had mine," Melody said as she sat at the table.

"And I can wait until later," Kaitlyn said.

"Okay." Dillon set his coffee down and sat in the chair across from Kaitlyn. He reached for the bear claw and hit Kaitlyn's hand instead. He glanced up at her, but she smiled sweetly.

"Sorry, they're my favorite too."

Melody chuckled a little and dropped her head as Kaitlyn brought the bear claw to her mouth and took a large bite.

All right, two can play that game. Dillon grabbed the eclair, his second favorite, and shot a pointed look at Kaitlyn.

"Oh, good morning everyone," Margie said as she entered the kitchen a few minutes later. Her sweater was black today but covered in puff paint that depicted a snowy scene. "I guess I overslept. I'm sorry I didn't have breakfast ready for you." She shot Dillon a loaded look. They had planned for his mother to be late to hopefully give him some time alone with Kaitlyn. It had worked. Sort of.

"No worries, Margie, but now that we're done maybe you can tell me where the Christmas decorations are. I'd like to get the room decorated today." Kaitlyn balled up her napkin and turned her attention on Margie.

"Of course, dear. I keep them down in the basement. I'm

sure Dillon would be happy to fetch them for you and help you decorate the room afterwards."

"Oh, that's not necessary," Kaitlyn said. "The decorating, I mean. Melody and I should be able to handle it."

"I don't mind." Dillon pushed back his chair. "I'll start bringing up the boxes right away." He left the room and Margie turned to the stove to begin making breakfast for the rest of the guests.

❄

"WHAT IS HE DOING HERE?" Melody leaned across the table and whispered to Kaitlyn as her eyes shifted to the path Dillon had taken.

"I had no idea," Kaitlyn said, shaking her head. "He showed up yesterday when I was looking for decorations. What was I supposed to do?"

"Are you going to stay here with him?"

"I'm not sure what else to do. I don't want to drive back and forth every day, and if I stay in town, I'll cut into my profits." She dropped her head into her hands. "It's so hard seeing him though."

"Actually, I thought he was pretty easy on the eyes," Melody said with a smile. Kaitlyn's head popped up, and she glared at her friend. "Okay, I'm sorry. He is very good looking though."

"I know," Kaitlyn moaned.

"Box one," Dillon announced as he re-entered the room. A light sheen of sweat glistened on his forehead. "Only about nine more to go."

"You have to run a race to get this?" Kaitlyn asked.

"No, just climb stairs and a mountain of other things."

"Oh, right, sorry about that. All right, I guess we'll get started sorting so I can see what we can use and what we'll need to purchase."

"Sounds good, I'll head back down for another delivery. Just call me Saint Dillon." He flipped a little salute and then walked out the door.

"Handsome and nice? Why did you guys break up again?" Melody asked as she stared pointedly at Kaitlyn.

Kaitlyn shook her head. It was bad enough she had to be here with Dillon. She didn't need Melody pointing out his good traits. "Let's forget Dillon for the moment and see what's in here."

"Of course. Whatever you say boss." Melody picked up the trash as Kaitlyn hefted the box and carried it into the living room. She set it on the couch and opened the lid. Strings of lights greeted her from inside, and from the look of them, they had just been wadded into the box.

It was going to be a long day today decorating. Melody entered the living room, her blond hair pulled up in a ponytail. Kaitlyn handed her a portion of the string. "Guess we better get started and see if any of these still work."

"Morning, Mom," Jack said as he entered the living room, still in his pajamas and yawning.

"Morning, Jack. I'm afraid today's going to be a busy day for me, but maybe Margie can give you some work to do."

Jack shook his head. "That's okay, Mom. I've got my tablet. I can keep myself busy, but does Margie have some breakfast?"

Kaitlyn smiled. Jack was like a bottomless pit. He could eat breakfast and then like clockwork an hour later he'd be asking for a morning snack. She hoped it just meant he was growing, but it sure was hard to keep enough food in the house for him. "She probably will soon if she doesn't already. Why don't you go ask her?"

As Jack left the room and the girls began untangling the lights, Dillon showed up with another box. And then another.

By the time he had brought up the last box, they had spread out five different strings of lights.

"You sure you don't want my help?" Dillon asked.

Kaitlyn looked up and realized he hadn't been kidding about there being ten boxes. If they were all like this one, it would take them all day just to sort. Unless she let him help. "All right, you can help. Can you see if you can find decorations?"

"I am happy to help beautiful women," Dillon said with a smile.

Kaitlyn ducked her head to hide her blush. This job suddenly felt a lot bigger than she had planned on.

True to his word, Jack stayed out of her hair, and by mid-afternoon, they had sorted all the items and Kaitlyn had decided which they were going to use and which could go back in boxes. Now, they needed a tree.

"I can try to come back down tomorrow if you'd like," Melody said as her eyes jumped from Kaitlyn to Dillon.

Kaitlyn glanced at her watch and cursed her timing. Melody did need to head back, and as there was no way she could get a tree on her own, that left her going with Dillon. "No, don't worry about it. I'm sure Dillon and I can handle it, right?" Kaitlyn didn't want to be alone with him, but the faster she got the room done, the faster she could return home and forget Dillon Fields again.

"I'd be happy to."

"Are you sure?" Melody asked with a lowered voice. Though she leaned in, her voice was still loud enough that Dillon heard and Kaitlyn caught his smile before he turned his face.

"I'm sure. Go."

Melody stared at her a moment longer. "All right. Let me know if you need any more help."

"I will. Drive back safely."

"Call me," Melody mouthed and then she was gone.

Kaitlyn looked at Dillon and her mouth dried up. She couldn't go alone with him. He still affected her too badly.

Jack popped his head in the room. "Mom, are you done yet? I'm bored." His voice had that whiny timbre Kaitlyn hated, but she couldn't really blame him. He had been good all day.

Then inspiration struck her. "I'm not done yet, Jack, but would you like to go with Dillon and me to pick a Christmas tree?"

His eyes lit up and he bounced from one foot to the other. "A real tree? Like one we cut down from a forest?"

"Yep. Just like that."

"Yes, please."

"Wonderful." She turned to Dillon so she could watch his reaction. "Dillon, this is my son, Jack. Jack, this is an old friend of mine from high school."

No look of shock crossed Dillon's face so Margie must have told him about Jack. He leaned down and stuck out his hand. "How you doing, little man?"

"I'm not a man. I'm five."

Dillon smiled as he stood back up. "Oh, well, you could have fooled me. Think you could help me cut down a tree?"

"I'm not allowed to touch sharp objects," Jack said, his tone and expression serious.

Kaitlyn bit her lip to keep from laughing. "Why don't you go get your coat, Jack?"

"He's very literal, isn't he?" Dillon asked as Jack left the room.

"Well, he's five. Kids are pretty concrete at this age."

"Yeah, I guess I don't know much about kids. He's cute though." Dillon ran a hand through his hair, and Kaitlyn wondered if he was nervous or just unsure what to say. She realized she would probably feel similarly if he had been the one to show up with a kid.

An uncomfortable silence descended as they stared at each other, but thankfully Jack returned moments later.

"Well…" Kaitlyn was at a loss for words. "Shall we go?"

Dillon led the way to his truck and opened the door for her and Jack. Kaitlyn shot him a glance but climbed in after her son.

CHAPTER 6

Dillon stopped the truck outside the forest he had taken Kaitlyn to in their youth. He glanced at her out of the corner of his eye to see if she noticed. A wistful expression flitted across her face, and he thought back to the first time they had been here.

"What are we doing here, Dillon?" Kaitlyn turned to him, a quizzical expression on her face.

"Just trust me." He got out of the truck and then walked around to open her door. The snow fell lightly against his face.

She smiled up at him as he opened the door. "You've got snow in your hair." With a gentle touch, she brushed his hair. He caught her hand and pulled her out of the truck and to his chest.

"There's about to be snow in your hair too." He tucked a

strand behind her ear and leaned down to place his lips on hers.

"Funny, I don't seem to mind," she said when the kiss ended. "Now, really, what are we doing here?"

"Picking out a tree. Come on." Dillon grabbed a saw from the back of the truck, grabbed her hand, and pulled her into the forest. "Pick your favorite."

Kaitlyn smiled as she looked from tree to tree. Her finger tapped her lips as she took in each one. Then her eyes lit up, and she pointed at a tall, leafy tree. "That one."

"That one it is," Dillon said. He laid down in the snow and began to saw the trunk.

"Can I pick the tree?" Jack asked breaking up Dillon's daydream.

"Well, there are some parameters," Kaitlyn said, "but, yes, you can help pick a tree."

Dillon opened his door and hurried around to get Kaitlyn's before she opened it. She smiled up at him as he took her hand and helped her out. He fought the urge to pull her to his chest like he had so long ago. As she paused before pulling her hand back, he wondered if she was remembering the night too.

"Let's go, Mom." Jack had slipped out of the truck behind her and was hopping from one foot to the other.

"All right, Jack." As she took his hand and headed into the forest, Dillon grabbed the saw from the back of the truck and hurried after them.

"What about this one?" Jack stood in front of a short tree not much taller than himself. The branches weren't very full, reminding Dillon of Charlie Brown's Christmas tree.

"No, I'm afraid that one is too small. The tree needs to fill the living room."

Jack scrunched his little face and moved to another group of trees. "How about this one?" This time he pointed to a gigantic tree that would never fit in the living room.

"I'm afraid that one is a little too tall," Dillon said. "Try to find one just a little taller than me." Dillon stood just past six feet and the living room had a clearance of ten feet, so if they could find an eight foot tree, they would still have room for the stand and the star on top.

Jack looked at Dillon as if trying to memorize his size. Dillon saw Kaitlyn bite back a smile to his right. As Jack moved off, Kaitlyn scooted closer.

"He's probably going to ask you to stand next to every tree now. Literal, remember?"

"That's okay. He seems like a great kid. How come you didn't tell me about him?"

Kaitlyn sighed. "It's a long story, Dillon."

He opened his mouth to say more, but before he could, Jack called out to him. "Dillon, can you come over here, so I can see if this tree is tall enough?"

"Told you." Kaitlyn's face pulled into a slight smile.

Dillon returned the grin and moved over to where Jack

was. Jack looked from him to the tree and shook his head. "Nope. Not quite. How about that one?"

Dillon followed the finger and moved over to the other tree. Again, Jack narrowed his eyes but shook his head. "Nope. Try that one."

Stifling a chuckle, Dillon moved to the new tree. Jack clapped his hands. "Yes, this one. Mom, what do you think?"

Kaitlyn's lips pursed as she walked around the tree. "It is the right height. That's good. And it does appear pretty full and robust." She shook a few of the branches. "It appears sturdy. Jack, I think you've done it."

He pumped his fist in the air. "Yes, I knew I could." Then his smile faltered. "But how do we get it home?"

"That's what this is for, little buddy." Dillon held up the saw.

"Oh." His eyes widened as he watched Dillon closely.

Dillon situated himself in the cold snow and began sawing at the base of the tree.

"Watch out!" Dillon could tell from the way the tree was leaning that it was going to fall directly on Kaitlyn.

"What?" Before she processed what he had said, the tree fell into her, knocking her to the ground and pinning her underneath. "Dillon, help. I'm stuck."

Dillon tried to stop the laughter from escaping. He placed his hand over his mouth, but the image of her hands flailing on the sides of the tree was too much for him and the chuckle issued forth.

"Dillon, get me out from under here right this instant." Kaitlyn's voice now held a tinge of anger, so Dillon quickly rolled the tree off her. He held a hand out to her, but instead of taking it, she yanked him down beside her sending snow flying into his face.

"What did you do that for?" he asked as he wiped snow off his face. Now he was wet and cold on both sides.

"Because you deserved it. And so I could do this." She rolled over and pulled him into a kiss which warmed him down to his toes.

"How about you watch the way you cut it this time?" Kaitlyn's voice held a teasing tone, but Dillon didn't even mind. He was just pleased she was remembering the incident as well.

"I'll be careful, but watch when it starts to lean and move if you need to." The saw cut through the trunk and the crunching sound of bark breaking reached his ears. "Here it comes." With a resounding thud, the tree fell to the ground.

"Now what do we do?" Jack asked.

"Now, we take it back to the truck and on to the inn." Dillon handed the saw to Kaitlyn as he would need both hands to drag the tree back. He took a deep breath and hefted the tree up on his shoulders.

KAITLYN TRIED NOT to stare as she watched Dillon lift the tree. Though she couldn't see his physique under the layers of clothes, she knew what was there. The memory of the last time they had been here had flooded her mind as soon as they arrived and wouldn't seem to go away. They had been so happy and carefree then. Just two young people in love. If only they could have stayed that way.

She shook her head. No! Even though a part of her wished she and Dillon had ended up differently, she wouldn't trade Jack for the world and he wouldn't have existed if she and Dillon had stayed together.

"Think you can help me lift it into the bed?" Dillon's voice brought Kaitlyn back to the present and she placed the saw in the bed before coming to his aid. "Can you hold this end while I lift the front and put it in? We'll lose less needles that way."

"I don't see any needles," Jack said.

Kaitlyn smiled. "It's the green things on the tree, honey. They aren't really leaves on pine trees. They are called needles, and we want them to stay on the tree as much as possible."

"Oh." Jack nodded, but Kaitlyn wasn't sure he really understood.

She took the base of the tree from Dillon, grunting a little under the weight and then moved with him when he picked up the top. It wasn't pretty, but between the two of them, they managed to get the tree loaded into the back of the truck.

"Now it's time for my favorite part," she said as she climbed in the passenger side next to Jack.

"What's that?" he asked.

"Decorating, of course." She tapped his nose earning a smile and a chuckle from Dillon as he started the truck.

Kaitlyn stared out the window as Dillon drove thinking back over all the time she had spent here in high school. After her mother died, she wasn't sure she would find happiness again, but then Dillon had come into her life. And since her father spent so much time working, she had quickly been welcomed into the folds of his family.

Too quickly, they were back at the lodge. Dillon parked the truck and hurried around to open Kaitlyn's door. She found it sweet that even after all this time, he rushed to open her door.

"Can I help you unload the tree?" Julian asked as Kaitlyn stepped out of the truck.

He, on the other hand, unnerved her a little. Julian always seemed to appear at the most random times and out of nowhere.

"Absolutely. I could use a hand getting it in the lodge," Dillon said.

Kaitlyn took Jack's hand and watched as Julian and Dillon muscled the tree out of the truck bed and into the lodge.

"Are you excited to help me decorate?" Kaitlyn asked Jack.

"Yeah, I want to help hang ornaments."

"It's going to take a few minutes for them to get the tree up, so how about we see if Margie has any hot cocoa we can warm up with."

"Yes." He grabbed her hand and pulled her into the kitchen.

"Are you back already?" Margie asked. She stood behind the counter mixing some sort of batter.

"We are, and we were hoping you had some hot chocolate we could sip on until the tree is ready to decorate."

"Kaitlyn, I know it's been awhile but I have always considered you family. You don't have to ask to get cocoa."

A flush flared across Kaitlyn's cheeks and she dropped her eyes. "Thank you, Margie."

After boiling some water, she poured both herself and Jack a mug and they took them into the living room. Kaitlyn made Jack sit at a chair right by the front door where there was no carpet. The last thing she needed was a brown stain on the carpet with the photographer coming in two days.

"Well, I think we have it all set up," Dillon said. "I'll put the lights on and then you can decorate to your heart's content."

Margie appeared in the doorway. "You know what we need? We need some Christmas music."

"Oh, I think I remember seeing them in one of the

boxes." Kaitlyn set her mug down on the coffee table and began opening the boxes.

"Julian, would you be a dear and take the boxes Kaitlyn doesn't need back down to the basement?"

"Of course, Mrs. Fields." Julian moved to just a few feet from Kaitlyn and stared down at her. A strange feeling blanketed her. She had no reason not to like him, but something about him just unsettled her.

When she didn't find the CDs in the box she was looking through, she closed it and pushed it his direction. He picked it up and disappeared from the room sending a feeling of relief through her.

"Ah, here they are," she said as she opened the next box. Five Christmas CDs sat right on top. Kaitlyn picked them up and turned to Margie. "If you've got a way to play these, we have music for hours."

"What kind of host would I be if I didn't have a way to play music?" Margie took the CDs and walked over to the front desk. From behind it, she pulled an old boom box.

Kaitlyn laughed and looked to Dillon. "Perhaps we should bring your mother into the twentieth century. Remind me after the photographer leaves to get her a proper entertainment station."

"I'll help you install it," he said as he wrapped the lights around the tree.

A moment later, the silky voice of Kenny Rogers filled the room. Though the song was old, Kaitlyn couldn't help but sigh. Kenny Rogers and Dolly Parton's Christmas album had been one of her favorites growing up, probably because her mom had been such a fan. Before she died, her mother had played this album every year while they set up their tree, and Kaitlyn had continued the tradition, at least until she went to college. Then she forgot about it. She wondered if the CD playing was her own copy, one she had left the last Christmas she had spent with Dillon.

"All right, the lights are ready." Dillon stepped back from the tree and followed the cords to the outlet. He plugged it in and the tree illuminated the room.

"Woohoo." Jack clapped from his chair. "Can we decorate now?"

"Of course. Give your mug to Margie so you don't spill and come pick an ornament."

Jack bounded out of the chair and practically skipped to Margie. Kaitlyn was glad his mug must have been mostly empty or it would have sloshed all over the floor. With the mug safely in Margie's hand, he changed direction and bounded to Kaitlyn.

"Okay, Jack, so if the ornament has a loop, you can just hang it on a branch. If it doesn't, you can loop this silver hook through the hole and hang it that way." Jack nodded. His eyes were focused on the ornaments, so Kaitlyn could only hope he was actively listening. "Try not to hang too many ornaments too close together, okay?"

His eyes finally flicked up to hers. "Okay, Mom. Can I hang one now?"

Kaitlyn chuckled and nodded. "Yes, go ahead." She let him grab an ornament before she got one. As she lifted it out of the box, she looked to Dillon and Margie. "Are you guys going to help?"

Margie waved a hand. "I'm going to watch, but I'm sure Dillon would love to help." Kaitlyn did not miss the wink she tossed to Dillon.

"Sure. I'd love to." He selected an ornament from the tree and smiled at Kaitlyn.

Warmth flooded Kaitlyn and she turned to the tree to hide the flush she knew had stolen across her cheeks.

They placed the ornaments in silence for a time. Every once in a while, Kaitlyn stepped back to examine the tree from a designer's eye. As she knew he would, Jack grouped many ornaments together, and she would sneak in and move them around while he was selecting his next one.

Sometime during their decorating, guests began to file in and sit around the room watching the process. When Jack hung the last ornament, he turned sad eyes to Kaitlyn. "Oh, man, that was the last one."

"That's okay, buddy. It looks great. You did a good job. Didn't he?" Kaitlyn looked to the other guests who smiled and clapped.

"I just wish we had some more." He plopped down on the couch and dropped his head into his hands.

Kaitlyn tried not to smile. Though it was a silly thing to her, she knew it was a big deal to him. "Tomorrow, I have to wrap presents for the tree. You want to help?"

A tiny light flickered in his eyes, but he played it off. "Okay, I guess."

"Well, I feel like singing. Is anyone up for some carols?" Margie asked.

"That sounds fun." Kaitlyn loved singing and caroling was another tradition she had lost when she went to college. She was grateful for the reminder and promised herself she would continue after this year.

Dillon and a few other guests joined her and they gathered around the CD player. Margie switched the disc and soon Away In A Manger filtered through the speakers. The voices of the guests blended together, creating a beautiful melody. At some point, a few people paired up and began dancing. Dillon held out his hand to her. "Join me?"

Kaitlyn hesitated. She wanted to dance with him, but she was afraid the feelings she was already having for him would spiral out of control.

"Please." His brown eyes pleaded with her, and Kaitlyn's wall crumbled. She nodded and accepted his hand. When his arms wrapped around her, she was transported back in time to their senior prom.

"Did I tell you how beautiful you look tonight?" Dillon asked as his arms tightened around her waist.

She smiled up at him and moved her hands from his

chest to wrap around his neck. "You clean up pretty nice yourself." As the music continued to play around them, Kaitlyn let her mind wander to their future. If she became a designer and he a photographer, then perhaps they could even have a business together where he took pictures of rooms and houses she decorated. She could almost see their son and daughter both with dark hair running around their feet as they tried to work.

"You did a wonderful job." Dillon's voice broke into her memory and the image of their children faded away.

"What?"

"With the room, the tree. Everything is beautiful."

"Oh, thank you."

"But not as beautiful as you."

Kaitlyn's eyes flicked up to meet his. "Dillon..."

"No, let me get this out. I made a mistake, Kaitlyn. Leaving you. I thought I wanted to see the world, and it was amazing, but I've come to realize that something is missing in my life. And that something is you."

Kaitlyn's mouth dried up, and she tried to reign in her feelings which were flying back and forth. Elation, fear, joy, disbelief. She felt like a snow globe all shaken up. "Dillon, I've missed you too, but I'm not the same person I was then. I have Jack to think about. I can't just jump into something without thinking of him."

Dillon's fingers grazed her cheek as he brushed a strand of hair from her face. "I understand that. All I'm asking for is a chance. A chance to talk, to see where we both are and where we could go together."

Kaitlyn glanced to the couch, but Jack had fallen asleep. His little hands were folded under his chin and his knees were curled to his chest. He looked younger than his five years. "I'd like that too, but not tonight. I need to get Jack to bed, and I need to figure out how I feel."

Sadness clouded Dillon's eyes for just a moment, but he nodded. "I can understand that. Would you like me to carry Jack to your room for you?"

"He's pretty heavy," Kaitlyn said with a smile.

"I don't mind."

"Okay."

Dillon dropped his arms and led the way to the couch. He carefully picked up Jack whose head rolled against Dillon's chest. Jack issued a small moan but didn't wake as Dillon climbed the stairs and laid Jack on the couch in The Sunshine Room.

Kaitlyn followed him back into the hall, closing the door behind her. "Thank you. We can talk again soon."

CHAPTER 7

K aitlyn looked through her bag one more time. She could have sworn she brought her locket with her but it was nowhere to be found.

"Mom, come on. I'm hungry." Jack had given her a full five minutes before beginning his morning whine. Now he stood at the foot of her bed holding his stomach as if he would keel over any moment.

"Just a minute, bud. Do you remember if I brought my locket?"

"I don't know, Mom. Can we go eat now?"

"I suppose." She pawed through the bag one more time and sighed. Maybe she hadn't brought it with her, but she was almost positive she had.

"Good morning, Kaitlyn, Jack," Margie said as they

entered the kitchen. "How do cinnamon rolls sound for breakfast?"

Jack's eyes danced. "Delicious, but are they almost ready? I've been starving for hours."

"Oh, it wasn't that long, Jack. Hey, Margie, no one has turned in a locket, have they?"

"No, I don't think so. Did you lose one?"

Kaitlyn helped herself to a mug of coffee. "Yeah, the one my mother gave me. I'm almost sure I wore it here but took it off the day we painted. I thought I left it on the dresser in the room, but now I can't find it."

"Oh dear. Well, no one has brought it to me, but I'll ask the other guests to look and I'll certainly keep an eye out for it."

"Thanks. I'll leave you my address before we head out today, so you can send it to me if you find it."

Jack looked up from the table. "We're leaving today? I don't want to go yet."

Kaitlyn added a little cream and then joined Jack at the table to wait for the cinnamon rolls. "I have to get back to work, Jack."

"You can't leave before the photographer gets here," Margie said adding her two cents to the conversation. "I'm sure he or she will want to meet the decorator who did such a wonderful job."

Kaitlyn looked from her son to Margie and rolled her

eyes. "Fine, I guess I'm outnumbered. We'll stay until the photographer gets here."

"Actually, since that will be tomorrow and the day after is Christmas Eve, you really should just stay until after Christmas," Dillon said from the doorway.

Kaitlyn hadn't heard him approach and she turned to him now with a small smile. "Not you too."

He shrugged and walked to the cabinet to grab his own mug.

"Please, Mom?"

Three pairs of eyes looked expectantly at Kaitlyn, and she threw up her hands. "Fine, but only through Christmas and then I have to get back to work."

"Well, since you did such an amazing job, I could give you more work here at the lodge. I need to redo the guest rooms you know." Margie smiled at her as she placed the cinnamon rolls on the table.

"I can sketch up some designs after I wrap presents today. I was just going to wrap empty boxes, but as it appears I'll be here through Christmas, I suppose I'll go shopping today."

"Can I come too?" Jack asked as his eyes roamed over the rolls. Kaitlyn knew he was looking for the biggest one.

"Sure, you can come." She picked a roll for herself and placed it on her plate. The heavenly scent of cinnamon and sugar floated up to her nose. She shouldn't be eating this; her pants already felt a little tighter, but she could get back to her workouts in a few days.

"I'd be happy to drive you." Dillon caught her eye as he sat down across the table from her.

"Why not? The more, the merrier. Would you like to come too, Margie?"

"No, I've got things to do around here, but I might give Dillon a list of things to get for me."

"Be happy to, Mom."

As Margie disappeared to take food into the dining room for the other guests, a silence fell on the trio. Kaitlyn dropped her eyes to the cinnamon roll unsure what to say to Dillon, especially in front of Jack. Dillon must have felt similarly because every once in a while she would see him look at her as if he wanted to say something, but then he would close his mouth and shake his head ever so slightly.

"I'm all done, Mom. Can we go now?" Jack asked as he finished his cinnamon roll. Icing and sugar was smeared across his face and coated his fingers.

"Go wash up and by the time you're done, Dillon and I should be ready."

Jack nodded and bounded out of the chair. When he was out of the room, Kaitlyn took the moment to clear the air. "While we're out, Dillon, let's not say anything about last night. I want to talk more, but not in front of Jack."

Dillon nodded. "As long as we get a chance to talk before you leave."

"I promise."

DILLON WATCHED Kaitlyn as she scanned the shelves of the store. She was so beautiful, and she deserved something amazing. The question was…. What? Back in high school, he would have known exactly what to get her, but now it had been so long. He moved over to a jewelry case, and a charm bracelet caught his eye. He could get her charms that represented her interests from high school and then he could add more as he got to know her better. It was the perfect gift.

"Can I help you with something?" One of the salesmen had approached while Dillon was scanning the case.

He looked up to make sure Kaitlyn was out of ear shot. "Can I get that bracelet?"

"Ah, yes, that is beautiful. Will you be needing some charms?"

"Yes please. Can I have the music note, the paint pallet, and do you have something that represents a mother?"

"Of course," the salesman pulled out the bracelet and the charms Dillon had already indicated, "how many children and what gender?"

"Just one. A boy."

"Then this one should be perfect." He held up a tiny charm of a mother holding the hand of a boy.

"Perfect." Dillon glanced up again, but Kaitlyn was on

the other side of the shop. "And how about one that represents love?"

The salesman followed Dillon's eyes and smiled. "Ah, yes." He pulled out a tray. "Here are the love charms."

Dillon scanned the offerings and pointed to one that called out to him. "That one. And can you please wrap them separately?"

"Of course, sir." The salesman totaled the order and while Dillon pulled out his credit card, the man began wrapping the delicate gifts. With the transaction finished, he handed Dillon two small boxes in a gift bag.

"Jack wants to play in the snow. Can you take a break?" Kaitlyn's voice came from just behind his right shoulder.

"Yep, all done. Let's go."

He followed her out to the little park area in the center of town. It was a perfect enclosed area for kids to play in the snow while their parents sipped coffees or nibbled on treats at the nearby tables.

As Jack ran over to some other kids, Dillon and Kaitlyn grabbed a nearby table and sat down.

"I thought this would give us a chance to finish our conversation from last night," Kaitlyn said.

"I'd like that."

"You might not like all of it, but here goes. When you left to go travel the world, I believed you would come back and we'd end up together, but as time went on, I began to realize you were never coming back. I can't say it did wonders for my self-esteem."

Dillon cringed. He had never really thought about how his actions affected Kaitlyn.

"I was pretty low when I met Jerry, and at first, I thought he was everything I was looking for. We got married and for a time everything was okay, but once I got pregnant, he began to change. He grew angry and began to yell. After Jack was born, the abuse turned physical and I knew I had to get out of there. Thankfully, he didn't fight me for a divorce - I think he just never wanted to be a father - but Jack has never really known his father."

"I'm so sorry, Kaitlyn."

She shook her head. "I don't tell you this for sympathy. I tell you because I have a feeling Jack will attach himself to the first male figure in his life. It's why I have to be sure before we start dating."

Dillon glanced over at Jack who was building a snowman with another boy. Was he ready to be a father figure? He hadn't been ready to propose, but he was sure that had more to do with Shana than being ready to be married.

"Kaitlyn, I don't guarantee what kind of father figure I'll be, but what I can say is that I've been comparing every woman I've dated to you over the last ten years. And all of them have fallen short."

She smiled and ducked her head. Dillon reached over

and grabbed her hand. Her eyes flicked up to his, but she didn't pull her hand away. They sat in silence, watching Jack play and enjoying each other's company.

A few minutes later, Jack bounded over to them. Kaitlyn dropped Dillon's hand before he got too close. "Mom, can we get some hot chocolate and a pretzel?"

"I suppose we can do that. Do you have anything else you need to get for your mother?"

Dillon pulled out his list and scanned it. He had bought everything his mother had asked for plus his gift for Kaitlyn. "No, I have everything I need. How about you?"

"Yep, I'm good too. Feel like a snack then?"

"Have you ever known me to turn down a soft pretzel?" It was the one snack he and Kaitlyn had fought over when they were dating in high school.

"You looked great tonight," Kaitlyn said as she ran up to Dillon after the game. She looked even better, and he wanted to kiss her, but she held in her hand his kryptonite. The smell of the soft pretzel assaulted his nose and sent his stomach rumbling. He hadn't eaten in hours and after running back and forth on the field, his hunger had intensified.

"Thanks, babe. And I see you brought me some food. That was so thoughtful. You must have known I was starving." He reached for the pretzel, but she moved her arm away.

"Not on your life. This is mine." She flashed him a wicked smile as she leaned back and took a giant bite.

"You little -" He grabbed her arm, pulling her close. As she fell into his chest, her arm neared his face and he snatched a bite from her pretzel.

"Hey, that was mine," she said as she pulled her arm away and batted his chest with her other hand.

He grinned at her as he finished chewing. "Thank you for sharing. Next time, buy two."

She narrowed her eyes at him for just a moment before tearing the pretzel in half and giving part to him. He took the pretzel but before he ate it, he pulled her close once again and kissed her.

She never bought just one pretzel after that time, or if she did, she ate it before coming up to him.

Kaitlyn rolled her eyes. "This time, you get your own," she said with a laugh. "Come on."

It warmed his heart that she seemed to remember the incident as well, and he stood and followed her to the bakery. He wanted to grab her hand again, but she had made it clear that she didn't want to do anything in front of Jack. At least not yet. He would respect that, but it didn't keep his heart from beating into overtime at the thought of kissing her. Nor did it stop the jolt of electricity that shot down his legs when the wind blew just right and the smell of vanilla from her body wash tickled his nose. No, it didn't stop those things at all.

After the pretzels were bought and eaten, the trio returned to the truck and made their way back to the lodge.

Dillon was surprised to see Julian waiting for them as they pulled into the parking lot. He hurried to Kaitlyn's door before Dillon could turn the truck off.

"Why, thank you, Julian," Kaitlyn said as he opened her door and held out a hand. "To what do I owe this gesture?" Though her words were kind, Dillon could hear the hesitation in them as she took Julian's hand and climbed out of the truck.

Dillon had no idea what Julian's angle was, but he hurried out of the truck and to her side just in case.

"Ms. Fields told me you were missing your locket. I looked around today and found it near the tree. It must have fallen off while you were decorating." He held up the necklace but made no move to give it back.

"Oh, thank you, Julian."

Kaitlyn held out her hand, but Julian smiled down at her. "I could help you fasten it if you like."

"Oh, um, well, all right." Kaitlyn turned her back to Julian and lifted her hair. Her eyes displayed her discomfort as she caught Dillon's gaze. Julian, on the other hand, smiled as he placed the necklace around Kaitlyn's neck.

Dillon forced himself to keep his hands at his side. A part of him wanted to knock Julian's hand away, so he could fasten the necklace himself. Like Kaitlyn, there was something about Julian that bugged him, but he chalked it up to jealousy. It was clear the groundskeeper was attracted to

Kaitlyn, but Dillon had finally found her again, and he wasn't about to lose her.

KAITLYN TRIED NOT to react as Julian's hands touched her neck. She was grateful he had found her necklace, but there was something about him that sent the tiny hairs on the back of her neck standing on end.

"Well, I better get these packages inside," she said when he finished. "They aren't going to wrap themselves."

"I'll help," Julian said as he stepped toward the truck bed.

"No need," Dillon said cutting him off. "We've got it covered."

Kaitlyn glanced at Dillon surprised by the hardness in his voice. Evidently he wasn't a fan of Julian's either.

Julian held up his hands and backed away. "All right, if you say so."

"Mom, can I get out now?"

Startled, Kaitlyn looked to the truck. Jack was still inside patiently waiting to be let out. The incident with Julian had shaken her so much, she had almost forgotten her son. "I'm so sorry," she said as she opened the door.

He shrugged as he jumped down. "It's okay. I'm glad you got your necklace back."

"Me too, buddy. Why don't you run inside while Dillon and I get the bags?"

"Okay."

As he bounded into the lodge, Kaitlyn turned grateful eyes on Dillon. "Thank you."

"No problem." He grabbed a few bags from the back of the truck and held them out to her. "I can tell he makes you uncomfortable."

Kaitlyn sighed as she took the bags. "I don't even know why. He seems like a perfectly nice guy. There's just something I can't put my finger on."

Dillon grabbed the last few bags. "Well, I for one don't like the way he looks at you."

"And how is that?"

Dillon glanced around before leaning close to her. "Like he wants to do this." He placed his lips on hers for just a second, but it was all the time she needed to know she wanted more.

As he pulled back, she looked up at him with a smile. "This is definitely a conversation I want to continue later, but I really do need to get these packages wrapped."

He grinned back at her. "Then I suppose we better head inside."

CHAPTER 8

K aitlyn looked around the completed room with a smile. It was beautiful if she said so herself. She'd had to move a few ornaments around, but the tree exuded perfection. With the presents expertly wrapped under the tree, It created a homey feel to the room and with the new furniture, it definitely belonged on a cover.

Dillon leaned closer and touched her hand. "It looks amazing. You did a wonderful job."

She squeezed his hand briefly and nodded. "This is going to be so great for your mother."

The front door to the lodge opened behind them, and they turned to see an unfamiliar woman with a black case slung over her shoulder enter followed by a trio of men holding lights and umbrellas.

"Hello. I'm Greta Schelling. I'm with Travel Magazine. Is Margie Fields around?"

Dillon stepped away from Kaitlyn and toward the woman. "I'm Dillon Fields, her son. I'll go get her for you." As Dillon headed into the kitchen, the photographer turned eyes on Kaitlyn.

"And you are?"

Kaitlyn cleared her throat and forced herself to speak up. "I'm Kaitlyn Bell, the decorator."

The woman's eyebrow arched as she surveyed the room. Her blond hair was pulled back in a ponytail, and her face held no emotion as her eyes moved from one side of the room to the next. When she had perused the entire room, the corners of her lips pulled up just slightly. "Yes, this place is beautiful. It will look lovely on our cover."

Relief flooded Kaitlyn. "Thank you."

But Greta had moved on. She turned to the men behind and began barking out directions for them to set up. Kaitlyn took a step back, not wanting to get in the woman's way. It was clear she was a "no nonsense" type of woman.

"Ah, Greta, I'm so excited to meet you." Margie entered the room with her typical flair. She had on a red dress trimmed in white and all her jewelry was Christmas themed. "I'm Margie Fields, the owner of this beautiful lodge."

Greta paused long enough to shake Margie's hand. "You've done a wonderful job with this room. I was just telling your decorator how good it will look on the cover. Do you have any other guests here now? I'd like to get a few shots of the room empty and then with people in it."

"Oh yes, we have a full lodge. The guests just didn't want to get in your way, but I can certainly round them up."

Greta flicked her slender wrist over and checked her watch. "Give me fifteen minutes." Then she turned back to the men and continued rapid firing her orders.

Margie glanced at Kaitlyn and Dillon before heading up the stairs to begin gathering the guests.

"She's rather intense," Dillon whispered in Kaitlyn's ears.

Kaitlyn nodded. "But maybe that's good. I bet it helps her get the best product."

They watched Greta take a few shots, move a few things around and take more shots. It was a fascinating process and Kaitlyn wondered if Dillon's job was similar, but she was afraid to ask him as Greta tensed every time something distracted her. Maybe intense wasn't even the right word to describe her. Vehement might be a little better.

A few minutes later, Margie returned with a few guests trailing behind her.

"Perfect timing," Greta said without even looking up. "Everyone please take a seat on the couches."

Kaitlyn and Dillon joined the others and took a place on the couch. Jack, who had entered with the other guests, sat between them.

The photographer scanned the room, and her eyes landed on Kaitlyn. "You. Yes, you, come here."

Kaitlyn glanced around to make sure Greta was speaking to her. The photographer motioned impatiently at her.

"Go on, Mom," Jack said pushing her.

Kaitlyn stood and walked toward the photographer, unsure of what she wanted.

"Stand there, please." Greta pointed to the side of the tree, and Kaitlyn acquiesced. Then she scanned the crowd once more. "Ah you. You come on this side."

Kaitlyn knew before she followed Greta's finger that she had pointed to Dillon, and her heart sped up in her chest.

"Yes, you stand on that side."

As Dillon followed the photographer's request, he lined up directly across from her. Their eyes met, and she tossed him a lopsided smile which he returned with a raised eyebrow.

"Now, I'd like you to reach for the same ornament. Let's make it that gold orb there." The photographer pointed to a gold ball directly in the middle of them.

Kaitlyn reached out her fingers and tried not to react when a tingle traveled down her hand as Dillon's fingers touched her own. Even after all this time, he still had the power to affect her.

"Yes, that is perfect." The camera clicked, but it was all background noise to Kaitlyn. Her eyes were focused on the man across from her. The man she had once loved and thought she had lost, but who God had placed back in her life. Could they make a go of this? Would he stay in Colorado or disappear again? Would Jack be okay if Dillon was in their life?

"Good. Now, you child, come join them."

Jack appeared next to Kaitlyn and waited for instructions.

"Stand in the middle," Greta said motioning with her arm, "and take a step forward. Now, you two come behind him. Make it look like a family."

Kaitlyn stepped behind Jack and Dillon joined her.

"Good. Now, Mom and Dad put your outer hands on the boy's shoulder." She paused for a moment as Dillon and Kaitlyn followed her directions. "Yes, now Dad, put your arm around Mom and Mom your arm about his waist."

Kaitlyn's heart hammered in her chest as she stepped a little closer and wrapped her arm around Dillon's waist. As his arm enveloped her shoulder, warmth flooded her body and the sense that this was home filled her.

"Perfect! Now smile." Greta continued to snap photos of them for another few minutes. Then she turned the camera on the other guests and snapped even more. "Okay, we have it. Let's wrap it up boys."

As quickly as she had come in, Greta packed up her equipment, shook Margie's hand one last time, and disappeared into the setting sun. It was so fast that Kaitlyn and Dillon hadn't even moved from their staged position. The guests all stared at each other for a moment, sharing a collected feeling of surrealness and then Margie burst out laughing.

"Well, I certainly expected a little more fanfare. I didn't even get to offer her cookies."

"I don't think she would have taken them," Kaitlyn said. Though she didn't want to, she was beginning to feel self-conscious still in Dillon's arms, so she dropped her arm and stepped just far enough way to create a space. He shot her a look, but said nothing as he dropped his arm.

"But I will." Laughter ensued at Jack's announcement and a chorus of agreement resounded from the guests. They rose and followed Margie into the kitchen leaving Dillon and Kaitlyn alone in the living room.

"I'm sorry I just want to wait until we talk…" Kaitlyn began.

Dillon shook his head, a smile on his face. "No need to apologize. We can talk more tonight. Shall we join the others?"

Kaitlyn nodded and followed him into the kitchen, thankful for the distraction even if it was only for a time.

IT WAS after nine that evening before they got to have their talk. Dillon waited outside Kaitlyn's door as she put Jack to bed.

"Sorry," she said as she stepped into the hall, closing the door behind her, "he took forever to go to sleep."

"No worries. I know it's cold, but do you want to go for a walk outside?"

A small smile played across her lips and she nodded. "Sure, just let me get my coat." She ducked back in the room for a minute, reappearing a moment later with a coat and scarf. "Okay, I'm ready."

Dillon grabbed his coat from his room and the two trekked down the stairs and out the front door. Snow fell lightly as they stepped onto the porch. Dillon grabbed Kaitlyn's hand smiling at her as she looked up at him.

"So, how do you see this working?" Kaitlyn asked. "I mean my life is here in Colorado, and yours is.... I actually don't know where you're living."

"It was Florida, but to tell you the truth, business hasn't been going so well. I'm thinking about changing things up."

"Things that might mean you'd be closer?"

"Indeed. In fact, I was thinking I might stay and help Mother for awhile. I know she's been busy ever since my father died."

"But what about after that? What happens when you are done helping your mother? I can't just pick up and move Jack."

"Kaitlyn, I get that you're scared, and I know some of that has to do with the way we ended, but I want to make this work. I'll do whatever it takes. If that means getting a job around here, I will do it." Dillon stopped and turned Kaitlyn to him. He took her other hand and held them to his chest.

"I want to believe you, Dillon, but you have to mean it. For Jack."

He cupped her face and stared into her eyes. "I do, Kaitlyn. I'm so sorry I hurt you then, and I'm even more sorry you married someone who hurt you, but I realize I've been searching for something the last few years and that something is you."

Her eyes glistened with unshed tears. "I've been looking for something too. Okay, let's give this another shot."

A surge of elation filled Dillon and he smiled before touching her lips with his own. Heat from the kiss flooded through him and the surrounding cold seemed to melt away. His heartbeat sped up as the kiss deepened and it took all of his control not to pull her back to his room.

"Oh, sorry, I didn't know anyone was out here." Julian's voice broke into the kiss and Dillon and Kaitlyn parted.

"It's fine. We were just taking a walk." Dillon didn't like the cold look in Julian's eye.

Evidently neither did Kaitlyn as her hand tightened on Dillon's and she turned to look up at him. "It's getting late. We should probably head back inside anyway."

Dillon nodded and regarded Julian one more time. "Have a nice night, Julian."

"You too." The words were pleasant but the coldness remained in his eyes.

Dillon didn't know Julian as he had been hired after Dillon left, but he would certainly be talking to his mother about him. The man gave him the creeps.

CHAPTER 9

C hristmas Eve had always been a fun filled day in the lodge and today was no exception. Margie had made a list of activities which Kaitlyn was scanning as she drank her coffee. Her eyes still felt heavy after her restless night. Though Jack had slept like a rock, images of Julian's icy stare had filled her vision and every floorboard creak had set her on alert.

"Good morning," Dillon said as he entered. He squeezed her shoulder before grabbing his own mug of coffee and joining her and Jack at the table. "Oh, the Christmas Eve schedule. This is when it gets exciting, Jack."

"I know. I want to do the sleigh ride and the popcorn stringing and the snowman contest. Can we do them all Mom, please?"

Kaitlyn smiled. Christmas Eve had been her favorite day

at the lodge when she was younger. Margie would always start with a morning snack of milk and gingerbread cookies. Then she would hold a sledding and snowman building contest. Lunch would be another huge affair with ham, sides, and pies for dessert. Then the sleigh would come and offer rides through the forest. A light supper of leftovers would be offered for any who still had room and then, when the sun set, they would sing carols and string popcorn. It never really made it on the tree as most of the kernels ended up in mouths, but it was fun nonetheless.

"Of course we can. It looks like she's added a coloring contest this year for the kids. Would you like me to see if I can get you one?"

"Naw, I think I'm too old to color unless the prize is cool. Is there a prize?"

Dillon chuckled. "I'll bet there is. Let me go find out. I'll even color one with you if you promise not to tell." He winked at Jack sending the boy into giggles before exiting the room.

"I like him. He's funny."

Jack's words hit Kaitlyn, and she took a deep breath. "Would you like to see him more often, Jack?"

The boy shrugged. "Sure. I'd come back here again."

"No, I mean back at our house. See, Dillon is a friend of mine from high school, and we thought we'd like to reconnect, so he might be coming around more often." It wasn't a lie, but Kaitlyn felt a little bad not telling Jack the whole truth.

"Will he play with me when he comes over?"

"I'm sure he will."

"Then I'm good with it." As if the conversation were finished, Jack turned back to his Lucky Charms and continued scooping them into his mouth.

Kaitlyn sighed. If only life were that simple. Dillon returned a moment later with three coloring sheets, crayons, and a wide grin.

"I brought one for you because I knew you'd get jealous," he said to Kaitlyn.

"You know me so well." In truth, she was pleased he had brought her a sheet. Coloring was an activity she enjoyed doing but rarely took the time to engage in.

"And I found out the prize is the golden stocking." Dillon placed a sheet in front of Jack and wiggled his eyebrows as he spoke.

"What is the golden stocking?" Jack's eyes were large and round as he stared at Dillon waiting for the explanation.

"The golden stocking is what one lucky person gets to hang every year. When Santa comes, he puts extra special surprises in that stocking, so someone is going to be very lucky."

"Oh, I hope it's me." Jack picked up a crayon and with a focus Kaitlyn rarely saw, he began coloring the sheet.

"I thought you were too old to color," Kaitlyn said with a laugh as she selected a red crayon for herself.

Jack paused and glanced up at her. "I am, but I am not too old for the golden stocking."

"Oh, right. My mistake." Kaitlyn grinned at Dillon as he sat down and picked up his own crayon.

As the trio colored in silence, Kaitlyn couldn't help but enjoy the feeling of family. It had been a long time since she had spent a holiday with her father, and she and Jack had left Jerry after the first Christmas, so the last four had just been her and Jack.

"Oh, good. I was hoping Jack would enter," Margie said as she entered with an armful of dishes from the dining room where the other guests ate breakfast.

"Do you need some help, Margie?" Kaitlyn hadn't minded not paying for her room when she was working, but now that the living room was finished and the cover picture taken, she felt a bit like a freeloader.

"That would be lovely, dear, if you don't mind."

"Not at all." Kaitlyn pushed back her chair and stood up. "Will you be all right for a minute, Jack?"

"Yep. I've got work to do." His nose was scrunched and the tip of his tongue stuck out between his teeth as he tried his best to stay in the lines.

Kaitlyn shook her head and pushed open the door to the dining room. The guests were all gone, probably enjoying their own Christmas Eve traditions, but Kaitlyn didn't mind.

She whistled softly as she picked up the Christmas themed plates and balanced them on her arm.

The first trip went without incident, but as she was picking up the last few pieces, the hairs on the back of her neck grew rigid. Someone was watching her. She turned slowly not fully surprised to see Julian watching her from the large bay window. Forcing a smile on her face, she waved with her free hand and hurried back to the kitchen.

Margie was rinsing the plates in the sink, and Kaitlyn handed her the last few items. She wasn't sure it was her place, but she had to know if Margie knew anything. "Margie, what do you know about Julian?"

"Julian? Well, I know he's very helpful and sweet. Wouldn't hurt a fly. Why do you ask?"

Kaitlyn bit her lip. She didn't want to start trouble if she was overreacting. "He just seems to be always watching me and, to be honest, he kinda scares me."

"Oh, I think he might have a little crush on you, but he's harmless." Margie placed the last dish in the drainer and dried her hands before turning to the cabinets and gathering ingredients for the cookies.

The words should make Kaitlyn feel better. After all, Margie knew him much better than she did, but somehow it didn't ease her worry.

"What do you think, Mom?" Jack held up his picture. At just five, he wasn't adept at coloring in the lines, but this was the best she had ever seen him do. He must have really buckled down and concentrated.

"It's beautiful, honey. I guess I'll have to finish mine later."

"No, you can color now. I still need to fix a few things."

"Oh, okay then." Kaitlyn took her seat again and shared a smirk with Dillon who was still coloring his sheet as well. He was earning definite points. Not many men would color with a five year old.

Silence fell between the three and soon the smell of gingerbread cookies filled the air. The trio finished their pages just as the oven timer dinged signaling the first batch of cookies was done.

"Who's ready for a snack?" Margie opened the oven and the warm scent of ginger filled the room.

"Me. I just finished coloring and that took a lot of concentration. I think I might even need two cookies." Jack flashed his most charming smile.

Margie raised her brow. "Two cookies, huh? You might have to clear that with your mother first."

Jack turned his pleading eyes on Kaitlyn and turned out his bottom lip in a small pout. "Please Mom." With his big, green eyes and long lashes, Jack was hard to resist.

"Okay, but only because it's Christmas Eve."

His lips pulled into a wide grin. "Thanks, Mom."

As Margie scooped the cookies off the baking sheet and onto a plate, Dillon grabbed the milk from the fridge and four cups from the cabinet. He filled each one and handed them out at the table. Margie set the plate of cookies in the middle and handed each one a red napkin with a tiny Christmas tree decal in the corner. Tiny wisps of steam curled up from the cookies and disappeared.

"Careful, they're hot," Margie said as Jack reached for the plate. He pulled his hand back and looked to Kaitlyn.

Careful not to burn her own fingers, she selected two cookies and placed them on the plate for him. "Be sure to blow on them first." He nodded and began puffing air on the cookies.

Kaitlyn chuckled as she grabbed a cookie for herself. After a few cooling breaths, she took a bite. The warm cookie melted in her mouth. There was just something about the taste of gingerbread that felt homey and safe.

DILLON ENJOYED the taste of the cookie, but more than that, he relished watching Kaitlyn's face. He wasn't even sure she knew she did it, but when she fancied the food she was eating, her eyes closed and a blissful look stole across her face. In high school, he had often teased her that she ate food seductively. Most people ate strawberries or ice cream in a seductive manner - it was hard not to when your tongue and teeth were so involved - but Kaitlyn did it with almost everything she put in her mouth. He had always been fascinated by how expressive her face was when she ate. Not that it wasn't expressive at other times, but it was different, more controlled.

"All done, Mom. Is it time for the snowman building contest?" A sprinkling of sugar that dusted Jack's mouth sparkled in the light as he turned to Kaitlyn.

"Um, I don't know. Margie?"

"Well, I have to serve the other guests their milk and cookies first, but you could get started. This contest isn't a timed one anyway. It's based more on creativity."

"All right, let's do it."

"Easy, tiger, let's get you bundled up first," Kaitlyn said. Her eyes raised to meet his. "Will you be joining us, Dillon?"

"Of course, I wouldn't miss it for the world."

Ten minutes later, they were bundled and stepping into the white wonderland.

"Look, there's our old snowman." Jack pointed excitedly at a large lump of snow that still vaguely resembled a snowman. Fresh snow and a bit of wind had shifted the shape quite a bit.

"You've done this already?"

Kaitlyn shrugged. "We had some time a few days ago."

A bit of awe filtered through Dillon as he registered the size of the mound. "It's taller than you are. How did you manage that?"

Kaitlyn shuddered and rolled her eyes. "Julian. He

appeared out of nowhere like usual and helped us. I know it might be easier to salvage, but I'd almost rather start fresh."

"I can't say that I blame you. I know Mother says he's harmless, but something just seems off."

She nodded and rubbed her arms. "Tell me about it. Hey, Jack, come on back. We can't use that guy. We have to start a new one."

"Why?"

Dillon jumped in to back Kaitlyn up. "Sorry, buddy, it's in the rules. The snowman has to be built on Christmas Eve to qualify."

"Aw, nuts." Jackson kicked at some snow but made his way back toward them.

"Thank you," Kaitlyn said.

"We're a team, remember?" He winked at her wishing he could hold her hand but willing to wait until she felt comfortable showing affection in front of Jack.

When Jack reached them, they began rolling the snow. Dillon was determined to make this snowman even bigger than the one Julian had helped with. It was petty, but he couldn't help feeling the need to be better.

As they finished the first ball, other guests joined them in the backyard. Soon, the quiet stillness was broken with the sound of laughter as some decided it was more fun to throw snow than mold it.

"We might win this one too," Jack stated, but there was a

wistfulness in his voice as if he wished he was throwing snow too.

"Why don't you go join in?" Kaitlyn suggested. "Dillon and I can finish here."

His eyes widened. "Really? Can I?"

"Yes, go. Maybe we'll even join you when we're done."

He didn't wait for any more affirmation. As fast as his little legs would carry him, Jack rushed over to the group throwing snow and began tossing his own bombs.

"You sure you want to be alone with me?" Dillon asked, a teasing smile tugging at his lips. "It could be dangerous as I've been thinking about kissing you all day."

"Me too." She glanced back at Jack. "I'll talk with him tomorrow after we open gifts. I hinted at it today, and he seemed fine, but I don't want to shock him."

Dillon understood, but he was looking forward to tomorrow evening when he could touch her without worry. "Hey, let's do dinner the night after Christmas in town. It'll be like a second first date. Mom could watch Jack, and we could have some time alone. I'll even let you pick the restaurant."

"Oh, how very thoughtful of you." Kaitlyn smacked him on the arm, but she was grinning. "I'd like that."

So would he. They shared a longing glance for a moment longer before turning their attention back to the snowman. When they finished, Dillon was pleased to see that not only was their snowman taller, but he seemed more proportionate as well.

They watched Jack play a little longer until he came over to them, shivering and red. "I think I'd like to warm up, Mom."

"Me too," she said. "How about we go in and warm up by the fire?"

Jack agreed, and they trooped back in the lodge, peeling off layers as the warmth hit them. After lighting a fire in the living room fireplace, the three sat on the largest couch. Jack curled up in Kaitlyn's lap and Kaitlyn leaned against Dillon. His arm wrapped around her shoulder and though he tried to keep his eyes open, the warmth and security of having her against him won out.

THE ROOM WAS DARKER when Kaitlyn opened her eyes. Jack was still snuggled on her lap and Dillon had an arm wrapped around her. As she moved to ease the ache in her back from the awkward position, Dillon groaned.

"Hey, you." His voice was still heavy with sleep.

She turned to look up at him. "Hey yourself. We must have slept a while."

"Wish it could be longer. I sure miss having you in my arms."

Kaitlyn glanced down at Jack, but his eyes were still

closed. She turned back to Dillon, and her voice was soft as she answered, "Me too." Then, with her free hand, she reached behind Dillon's neck and tugged bringing his head to where she could lean up and taste his lips.

"Mmm, and I definitely miss that."

Kaitlyn was about to agree when Jack stirred in her lap. "Is it time for stockings yet?"

"It might be. We need to find Margie and see."

"Did someone mention my name?" Margie's voice carried over from behind the couch. "I was wondering if you three were going to sleep all day." Her face appeared at the back of the couch.

"Sorry, Margie, I guess building the snowman wore us out."

"Oh, no worries, however, everyone else has eaten, so if you're hungry I can make some leftovers and we can do stockings after that."

"That sounds great, Mom."

The three followed Margie into the kitchen and sat at the table as she heated up ham, sweet potatoes, and rolls. After a quick prayer, they dug in. Kaitlyn hadn't realized how hungry she was until her plate was empty. Dillon and Jack must have been as well as they finished shortly after her.

"Now is it stocking time?" Jack asked looking from Kaitlyn to Margie.

"Yes, now it can be stocking time," Margie answered

with a smile. "Why don't you head back into the living room? I'll get the stockings and the rest of the guests."

"Let's put our plates in the sink first," Kaitlyn said shooting Jack a look. "We can clean up after ourselves, right?"

He nodded and took his plate to the sink. Kaitlyn and Dillon followed suit before heading back into the living room. A few minutes later, the rest of the guests filed in. Kaitlyn smiled at each one until Julian entered. Then, her smile faded. His eyes held hers for a moment and something tugged at Kaitlyn's brain. She closed her eyes to try and focus, but nothing clear came. Only the same feeling of unease.

"Okay, everyone, I have the stockings and the winners." Margie's entrance dispelled the nagging twinge and Kaitlyn pulled Jack to her. "I have two gold stockings this year. Our first winner for the coloring contest is Megan."

Jack's shoulders slumped under Kaitlyn's arm as a girl, probably around twelve, made her way to Margie.

"It's okay, buddy. You did a great job." Kaitlyn's heart broke at the sight of his sad face, and she sent a tiny prayer up that they would win the snowman contest. Perhaps it was silly to pray for something so small, but nothing that saddened your children was small when you were a parent.

Megan hung the gold stocking on the farthest hook and then sat back down.

"Our next winner is…" Margie paused and looked

around the room dramatically, "Jack, for the wonderful snowman."

Kaitlyn squeezed his arm. "See? I told you."

As Jack stood to get his gold stocking, Kaitlyn felt eyes on her. She turned to see Julian staring at them. His arms were crossed and his expression appeared angry.

Jack hung his gold stocking next to Megan's and then Margie handed out the rest of the stockings and the rest of the children hung them on the remaining hooks.

"Now, who wants to string some popcorn?" Margie asked.

The children shouted and followed her into the kitchen and soon the smell of popcorn filled the air.

"Shall we go string some popcorn?" Kaitlyn asked. Though she enjoyed the Christmas tradition, she wasn't sure she wanted to move. It was nice having Dillon right next to her.

"I suppose we better." His arm stole around her and caressed her shoulder. "Though I don't really want to move."

"Me either," she whispered snuggling into him. "Maybe we can stay like this for a few more minutes."

"Fine with me." He kissed the top of her head and inhaled.

Kaitlyn turned her face up to his. "Are you smelling my hair?"

A tiny twinge of pink colored his face. "I was. I always loved the way your hair smelled."

"I guess that makes two of us." She twisted so they faced each other and slid her hands up into his hair. "I've always loved the way you smell too."

Their gazes locked and her heart sped up as he leaned down, but before their lips could touch, Jack burst into the room. "Come on, Mom. The popcorn is ready."

With a sigh, Kaitlyn whispered, "To be continued," to Dillon before turning to face Jack. "All right, buddy, we're coming."

CHAPTER 10

Dillon woke as the first rays of sunshine poked in his windows. He wasn't generally an early riser, but he had always loved Christmas, at least when he was growing up. The last few years, he could barely even remember celebrating it.

Flicking back the covers, he stood and padded over to the dresser where he had hidden Kaitlyn's gift. The charm bracelet he would give her today. The special charm, he was planning to save to give her at dinner tomorrow.

He opened the drawer and pulled out the wrapped box, but his eyes widened when the unwrapped box wasn't just beneath it. Dillon moved the other clothes around, but it was nowhere to be found. He was sure he had left it right under the other box, but if that were the case, where was it now?

Maybe he had taken it out to show Margie, but he didn't remember doing that. Could he have left it in his coat pocket? He ran a hand across his face. Well, worst case, he could pick up another in town tomorrow. Still, he couldn't shake the feeling that someone had been in his room and taken it. But why?

The question would have to wait until later. He could hear the stirrings of the fellow guests and knew present opening would commence soon, and he still needed to take a shower. Dillon set the box on the top of the dresser and headed into the bathroom.

Fifteen minutes later, he was clean, dressed, and anxious to give his gift to Kaitlyn. He hoped she loved it. He headed downstairs and to the kitchen first. As excited as he was, he still needed coffee.

"Good morning," his mother said as he entered. She was wiping off the counter and in her full Mrs. Claus outfit today - a red suit with white fur trip. "There's an excited little boy waiting on you."

Dillon chuckled. "I figured, but I had to shower first and get some coffee." He pulled a mug from the cupboard. "Hey, did I show you what I got Kaitlyn for Christmas?"

"No, what is it?"

"It was a special charm, but now it's gone. I thought maybe I had misplaced it after showing it to you though I didn't remember doing that, but I'm starting to wonder if someone took it."

His mother's brow furrowed. "Who would do such a thing?"

"I don't know." Dillon took a sip of the coffee, "but I plan to find out." He grabbed one of the cinnamon rolls his mother had made, wrapped it in a Christmas napkin, and headed to the living room.

"He's here now, Mom. Now, can I open my presents?"

Kaitlyn rolled her eyes at Dillon behind Jack's back. "Yes, now you can open your presents."

"Yay." Jack made a beeline for the tree and began examining each box under the tree.

"Can he read yet?" Dillon asked as he set down his coffee on the end table and sat down on the couch. "Because if not, this could get messy."

She chuckled and grinned at him. "He can read his name."

"Look, Mom, who's this one from?" He brought over a large box wrapped in green and red plaid.

Kaitlyn leaned forward to read the tag. "That is from Margie. Ah, she didn't have to do that."

"Yes, she did," Margie said from the doorway to the kitchen. "I miss being able to buy things for young ones. Heaven knows my only son is taking his time providing me grandchildren to spoil."

"Mom," Dillon admonished, but he enjoyed the blush that spread across Kaitlyn's cheeks. Funny, they hadn't had that talk yet. Unless you counted the one they'd had in high school.

Kaitlyn swung his hand back and forth as they walked. Autumn leaves crunched under their feet but it was just warm enough they only needed a light jacket. "So, how many children do you want when we get married?"

"Married?" Dillon tried not to choke on the word. He had just turned eighteen, and while he believed he loved Kaitlyn, he hadn't thought about marriage.

"Don't look so shocked, Dillon Fields. I plan to marry you one day. Not any time soon, but one day, and I want to make sure we're on the same page."

That should make him feel better. She wasn't planning on rushing into anything, but somehow it didn't. He would be graduating soon, and his thoughts were consumed with photography and traveling, not children. "Oh, I don't know, one of each?"

"Only two?" Tiny lines appeared in her forehead as her face scrunched. "I want more than two. It was so lonely growing up an only child. Weren't you lonely?"

Dillon shrugged. Though he also was an only child, there had always been people at the lodge his family owned, and most of the time there were other children. He hadn't often felt alone.

"Oh, I guess with all the guests you probably weren't. Well, I was. It was just my mom, dad, and me. Then when

Mom died, it was just Dad and me. I don't want my kids to feel like that. I think we should have four at least."

"Four?" His throat was drying up again.

"Well, yes, two is too few and three is odd. What if we have two boys and only one girl or vice versa. The odd one out would get lonely, but with four there's two of each."

"You do know it doesn't always work like that, right? There was a family who stayed with us once who had ten children. Nine boys and only one girl."

Kaitlyn shuddered. "Ugh, I always wanted a brother, but nine of them? That seems a little much. Anyway, I know God will provide exactly the number we need when the time comes."

Dillon nodded, but he was glad when the conversation ended and moved to less heavy topics.

Yep, they should have that conversation soon. He wanted to know if she still wanted four and let her know that he was willing to have at least three. Hopefully, they could meet in the middle.

Jack pulled off the paper to reveal a remote train set. "Wow, this is so awesome. Thank you, Miss Margie." The boy set the box down long enough to run and hug Dillon's mother. Then he was right back at the tree pawing through packages.

"Who's this from, Mom?"

Kaitlyn smiled. "That one is from me. See, this word is Mommy."

Something tugged on Dillon's heart as he watched the scene. He couldn't believe he hadn't entertained the thought of having children before, and at this moment, he would agree to whatever number Kaitlyn wanted.

"It's the game I wanted. Thank you, Mom."

"You're welcome. Now, you have more gifts from me back at our house. I hadn't expected to stay here this long."

"That's okay. I'm glad we did."

"Is it my turn now?" Dillon glanced down at the bulge in his pocket where the wrapped box was hidden.

"You have gifts too?" Jack asked. "How do you spell your name, and I'll look."

"Oh, I probably do, buddy, but I meant that I had a gift for your mother."

Kaitlyn's lips parted. "For me? You didn't even know you would see me."

"No, but once I knew you were here, I couldn't pass up the opportunity to get you something. It's nothing big, but I hope you like it." He pulled the box out and handed it to her.

"I didn't get you anything," she began, but he held up his hand.

"I didn't ask you to. Just open it."

Jack leaned against his mother's side, clearly curious as to her gift. Kaitlyn unwrapped the box and lifted the lid. Her eyes lit up as she pulled out the delicate bracelet. "It's beautiful, Dillon."

No longer interested, Jack sat on the floor and opened his toys.

"It doesn't even compare to you, but it's a start." Dillon reached for the bracelet and helped her fasten it.

Kaitlyn dropped her eyes. "I wish I had gotten you something."

Dillon lifted her chin with his finger. "Hey, you going to dinner with me tomorrow is gift enough."

The lodge door opened and Dillon and Kaitlyn both turned to see who it might be. Dillon's heart stopped in his chest when he realized it was Shana.

"Dillon! Oh, good, I did find the right place." She set down her suitcases and shut the front door. "I wasn't sure that driver knew where he was going when he didn't stop in town." Shana glanced around the room. "Well, this is …. Quaint." The tone of her voice didn't match her words however.

Dillon saw Kaitlyn stiffen and wished he could explain. He flashed her a look he hoped said It's-not-what-you-think and rose from the couch. "What are you doing here Shana?"

"I'm here to visit you, silly. It is Christmas after all."

"Yeah, but you said you hated the cold. And we broke up, remember?"

"Oh, I know you weren't serious about that, and after I saw this beautiful cover," she pulled out a copy of the Travel magazine, "I just had to come see this amazing place. How come you didn't tell me it was so beautiful?"

"You didn't ask." Frustration flooded Dillon. How dare she waltz in here and act like nothing had happened? "How did you even get that? I didn't think it was released yet."

"Oh, it isn't for the general public, but Greta is a friend of mine. When she realized you were *my* Dillon, she called me."

Behind him, Kaitlyn sucked in her breath and Dillon gritted his teeth. He would have to do major damage control later. "But I'm not *your* Dillon. Not any longer. I broke up with you."

Her mouth turned out in a pout. "But, Dillon, I heard through the grapevine you were ring shopping. You can't go from wanting to propose to breaking up."

"Come on, Jack, let's go play in our room and give Dillon some privacy," Kaitlyn said behind him. Her voice was cold and composed, and the knife twisted tighter in Dillon's heart.

"I didn't buy a ring, Shana. I realized as I looked at them that I had no idea what you would want."

"Oh, you know what I like." She batted her eyes and stepped toward him.

"No, Shana, I don't. I don't know if you like round or princess cut. I don't know if you prefer gold or silver. The only thing I realized I know about you is that you don't like cold places. And I realized I didn't love you, which is why I broke up with you."

"I like princess cut, a carat or more, and platinum. See? Now you know."

Dillon shook his head. "Where is this coming from anyway, Shana? You said you didn't want to meet my mother, that you weren't ready to commit."

"I just realized how much I missed you while you were gone." Which Dillon knew translated into the fact that she had been bored without him there.

"I'm sorry you came all this way, Shana, but we're not getting back together. See, after you decided not to come with me, I started thinking back to the last time I was really happy, and I realized it was in high school when I was dating Kaitlyn. I had no idea I would find her here, but here she was. It was like God was proving we belonged together, and she's the one I want to be with."

Shana's face hardened. "So, what am I supposed to do now?"

"Go home. Find someone who loves you as much as you love yourself. I wish you the best, Shana, but it's not with me."

"But it's Christmas Day, Dillon. I can't get anywhere until at least tomorrow. Perhaps I can just stay the night and we can talk about this later."

Dillon fought to keep control. She wasn't listening to him, and as much as he hated sending someone away on Christmas Day, he couldn't have her stay here. "Look, I'll call the other lodges in the area to see if anyone has a room.

If not, maybe we can figure something out, but regardless, there's no reason to talk any further because we are through."

KAITLYN TRIED NOT to stare as Dillon and the woman conversed, but when she stated Dillon had been ring shopping, the room began to spin. She knew she was close to having a panic attack though she hadn't had one in years. How could he have been shopping for rings for someone else and not have told her?

"Come on, Jack, let's go play in our room and give Dillon some privacy." She didn't want to go. She wanted to hear the rest of the conversation, but she didn't think she could handle it. Kaitlyn grabbed one of Jack's presents while he grabbed the other and they headed for the stairs.

"They make a cute couple, don't you think?"

Julian's voice came from the right where he leaned against the wall at the top of the stairs. Kaitlyn shot him a look, but she didn't want to engage him. She just wanted to get to her room and cry. Of course, she wouldn't be able to do that while Jack was awake, but maybe she could escape into a good book while he played and he wouldn't notice if a few tears spilled out.

"Excuse us." Kaitlyn pulled Jack past Julian and into their room shutting the door behind her.

"What's wrong, Mom?"

"Nothing, honey. Mommy just needs some time to think. Can you play quietly for a little bit?"

"Sure." He plopped down on the floor with his new game.

Kaitlyn rifled through her suitcase until she found the book she had been reading. She usually read on her phone so she could hold it in one hand and follow Jack around, but she always carried a paperback book when she traveled just in case. And this time, she needed the size of the book to hide her face.

She'd become adept years ago at crying silently. It had been the only way to release her feelings when she had been married to Jerry. The first time he had hit her, she'd made the mistake of crying out loud, which only made him madder. She'd walked with a limp for a week after that due to the bruising he gave her thighs.

Kaitlyn quickly learned to cry silently following that first beating. When Jerry got angry, he would yell, hurl insults at her, and occasionally his fists would make contact, but if Kaitlyn remained still, the onslaught was usually over within a few minutes. Then, she could retire to their room, roll over in bed, and let the tears flow down her cheeks. He was none the wiser, and her body didn't suffer as much.

With the book in front of her face, she let the tears fall. She had known things with Dillon would end badly. In fact, she had set rules to keep this very thing from happening.

Unfortunately, she had let her emotions cloud her judgment and broken the rules. How could he have not told her he was nearly engaged?

True, they hadn't had much time alone to talk, but looking at rings was pretty big. And this woman was clearly a model or something. She was gorgeous. Kaitlyn could never compete with that. She was more like the girl next door than the girl on the cover of a magazine. And it sounded as if this breakup was recent. She had no desire to be his rebound relationship. That never went well and rarely lasted.

Kaitlyn bit her lip as the words blurred. She wished Melody were here to talk to. Though Melody would probably start with 'I told you so.' Still, she would understand and maybe she would even have an encouraging word to say.

Perhaps she and Jack should just leave tomorrow. She could tell Margie she'd work on the rooms another time. She hadn't even begun designing them. Maybe that's what she should do: Whip out the designs the rest of today and tomorrow, leave them with Margie, and do the rooms after Dillon was gone.

The solid plan made her feel minutely better, and a few blinks cleared the remaining tears enough that she could actually read the page. Another deep breath calmed her heart, and she soon found herself immersed in the story. So much so that she didn't recognize the first knock at the door.

"Mom, someone's knocking." Jack had been taught from a young age not to open the door to strangers, so he generally just told her when someone was there.

"Hmm?" Kaitlyn looked up from the book as the knock sounded again. "Oh, right, coming." She placed her bookmark back and closed the book before crossing the room. As the door swung open, Kaitlyn realized she should have checked the peephole first. Dillon stood on the other side, and she wasn't sure she was ready to talk to him.

"Hi. I know you're probably angry, but I'd like to explain. Can we take a walk?"

Her shoulders rose with her breath as she debated. She probably should at least let him explain before she completely threw him off the bus, though she doubted it would help much. A glance back at Jack showed him engrossed in his game. "Jack, will you be okay if I take a walk with Dillon for a bit?"

"Sure, Mom." He didn't even look up from his tablet as he spoke.

"Okay, a walk, but this had better be good." Kaitlyn grabbed her coat and hat before following Dillon to his room so he could do the same. With coats donned, they headed down the stairs and out the front door. Though she wasn't sure she cared, Kaitlyn looked around for the stunning blond as they passed through the living room.

"Where's your fiancee?" she asked as they stepped into the cold afternoon.

Dillon sighed and shoved his hands in his pockets. "First, she is not my fiancee."

Kaitlyn shot him a look with raised eyebrows. Did he really expect her to believe that?

"Okay, yes, I did look at rings, but it was because I felt like I should not because I loved her. I realized when I had no idea what ring she would like that I shouldn't marry her. Then when I invited her to come here and she decided she didn't want to meet my mother or go anywhere cold, I knew I had to break it off. Honestly, I had been thinking I needed to end it for a couple of months, but that was the final straw."

"I'm not sure how to feel about that, Dillon. I don't want to be a rebound."

Dillon grabbed her arm and turned her to face him. "You are *not* my rebound. I told you that I couldn't stop thinking about you. After I broke it off with Shana, I thought back over my last few relationships and realized I broke up with all of them because they weren't you. So, if anything, those women were the rebound from you."

He had all the right words, but he always had. Even in high school, Dillon had been a smooth talker. But so had Jerry. Until his smooth words had turned into vicious insults. "I want to believe you, I do, but in the last ten years, I've learned words are cheap. Actions are what matter."

Dillon nodded. "I can understand that, and that's why I need you to know I sent her away. I drove her into town and dropped her off at another hotel. She'll be leaving tomorrow. Kaitlyn, I know it may take a while for me to prove this to you, but there's no one else for me. Watching you with Jack these last few days have driven that home even more for me. I want you in my life. I want Jack in my life, and I'll do whatever it takes to prove that to you."

Kaitlyn's emotional wall dropped a little. The earnestness was evident on Dillon's face. "Okay. I believe you, but, Dillon, my heart can't take this again and I won't crush Jack."

"You won't have to. I promise." With those words, he pulled her to him and though she still had reservations, she allowed him to kiss her and quiet them for the moment. She could only hope her faith wasn't misplaced.

CHAPTER 11

D illon woke the next morning with two things on his mind. One, he was going to replace the charm he had somehow lost. He'd dug through all the drawers after he and Kaitlyn retired last night, but still come up empty handed. Two, he was going to prove to her that he was committed.

They had planned dinner, but he wanted to make sure he got them in the nicest restaurant and had flowers waiting for her. The charm wasn't an engagement ring, but for him it was like a promise. If he could convince her he wasn't going anywhere, he could see marriage in their future.

He grabbed his clothes for the day and took them into the bathroom with him, whistling as he went. A hot shower would be the perfect start to the day. Then he could grab breakfast and coffee and head into town to take care of all the details. Hopefully, Kaitlyn would understand his absence.

He set his new clothes on the counter, stripped off his pajama pants, and stepped into the shower, turning on the faucets and adjusting the temperature until it was perfect. As the water pelted his skin, his mind pictured the future. He wanted to stay and help his mother with the lodge, but Denver, where Kaitlyn lived, was over an hour away. It wasn't a terrible commute, but it would be if he did it daily. Perhaps, he could convince her to move a little closer, but that would mean moving her business. Or, maybe he could get a job in Denver and help his mother out on the weekends. Though he didn't have all the answers, he knew he would figure them out.

As he turned off the shower, he heard a scuffling noise. His body tensed, and he grabbed the towel and wrapped it around his waist not bothering to dry off first. The immediate vicinity looked untouched and he took a deep breath before stepping toward the doorway to his room. Confronting a thief or an attacker wearing only a towel certainly didn't give him confidence. He looked around for a weapon to wield, but there was nothing.

He took a deep breath, pulled back his shoulders, and charged into the bedroom. The room was empty, but his door was ajar. Dillon knew it had been shut; he would never have stepped into the shower if the door were open. Which meant someone had been in his room. Someone with a key.

With quick strides, he crossed the room, opened the door, and poked his head out. The hallway was empty. Whoever had been there was gone now. He shut the door once again and engaged the lock. He would have to tell his mother about this after he dressed because unless she had been in here, Dillon was fairly certain the culprit was Julian. The question was, why?

He found his mother cooking pancakes at the stove when he entered the kitchen. "Morning, Dillon," she said as she glanced his direction.

"Morning, Mother. Were you in my room just a minute ago?" He grabbed a mug from the cupboard and filled it with coffee.

"No, I've been down here making breakfast. Why?"

Dillon glanced around to make sure Julian was nowhere nearby. "Mom, I think we might have to do something about Julian."

Her brows knitted together as she looked at him. "Julian? Whatever for? What does he have to do with this?"

Dillon added a few spoonfuls of sugar to his coffee and stirred it before leaning back against the counter. "I heard a shuffling noise when I was in the shower. By the time I got out, whoever it was had left, but my door was open, and I know I shut it before I got in the shower."

His mother shook her head. "But why would Julian be in your room?"

"I don't know, Mother, but first my gift to Kaitlyn went missing and now this? I don't think it's a coincidence."

She pursed her lips as she turned back to the pancakes. "He's so nice, and he's always been so helpful. I just can't believe he would do this."

"Well, I can't think of anyone else it would be. No one has the keys, right?"

"No, no one does." She scooped up the pancakes and placed them on the plate.

Suddenly an idea struck Dillon. "Hey, do you still have his employment paperwork? His resume or something with his social on it?"

"Of course. You know I keep meticulous records, but why do you need them?"

Instead of answering her question, he posed his own. "Does Dan still work for the police in town?" Dan had been a friend of his father's before he died. The two would often get together to bowl or shoot pool. At least that's what they told his mother. Secretly, Dillon thought they had snuck away to smoke cigars. His mother hated the smell and swore his father had given it up, but Dillon had found a humidor in his father's desk one day and decided bowling was a perfect ruse to come home smelling like smoke.

"I believe so, but I haven't spoken with Dan since your father passed."

"Good. Hopefully, he won't mind doing me a favor. I'm going to go into town later today to replace Kaitlyn's gift. I can stop by the station and see if he can give me any information on Julian."

His mother sighed and turned off the stove. "Is that really necessary?"

"Mom, if he's a thief, don't you want to know before he puts the lodge or those who stay here in danger?"

"I suppose, but it seems so drastic. Can you get some plates?"

Dillon did as she asked as she carried the pancakes to the table. "Look, if he comes back clean, I'll give it up and he never has to know. But if he doesn't," Dillon shrugged, "I'll help you find a new groundsman."

"It's not just that," she said with a sigh as she set the plate down and then pulled out a chair, "Julian's been here since just after your father died. He's like family."

As she sat down and dropped her head onto her hand, Dillon noticed for the first time the lines on her face. How had he not seen them before? His mother was lonely. He sat across from her and grabbed her hand. "Mom, I know I haven't been around much, but I'm going to be here a lot more."

Her shoulders lifted and hopeful eyes held his gaze. "What are you saying?"

"I'm moving back, Mom. Kaitlyn and I are getting back together, so I want to be close to her, and I've missed Colorado."

"But what about seeing the world?"

Dillon rolled his eyes. He had been everywhere. After high school, he had decided to backpack through Europe and taken tons of pictures there. Some of those shots had landed him jobs in Hawaii and the Caribbean. He had seen the world. Almost every country. "I've seen it, Mom, but it's always been missing something, and I think that something is Kaitlyn."

"Oh, I'm so happy." His mother squeezed his hand, a huge smile on her face. "But won't you miss being a photographer?"

"I'm not giving it up entirely. Just putting it on hold for a little bit. Besides, I can help you take pictures of the rooms after Kaitlyn redoes them and we can add them to the website to help drive up business. So, I'll still be doing what I love."

His mother stood then and enveloped him in a hug. "You've made an old woman so happy."

"Are we interrupting?" Kaitlyn asked from the doorway. Her face was scrunched in a comical expression as if she wasn't sure what to make of the scene before her.

"Absolutely not. Come in and join us. Dillon was just telling me the good news of him staying here."

"You get to live here?" Jack asked. His eyes widened and his jaw dropped. "You could build a snowman every day."

The adults all chuckled. "Well, only in the winter buddy, but yeah, I guess I could."

"You are so lucky. I wish I could live here."

As he climbed up in a chair, Dillon and Kaitlyn shared a look. Was she picturing a life here as he was?

"Well, how about we eat?" His mother asked as if she could sense the electricity in the air between Dillon and Kaitlyn.

"Yes, we're starved, and these look delicious," Kaitlyn said as she pulled out a chair next to Dillon.

After breakfast, he pulled Kaitlyn aside. "I'm going into town to run some errands. I'll text you with the restaurant name and the time to meet for dinner. Do you think you'll be able to drive there yourself?" Dillon knew she was a capable driver, but more snow had fallen since the last time she drove, and he wanted to make sure she arrived safely.

"I'll be fine," she said with a smile.

"Good. I'm sorry I'll be gone all day though."

She squeezed his arm. "Don't worry. I need to work on the designs for your mother today anyway. It's probably a good thing because I don't get much work done with you around."

As he pulled her in for a quick kiss, he thought about warning her about Julian, but her guard was already up where he was concerned, and Dillon wanted to be sure before he accused the man. However, he did stop by his mother's office and retrieve Julian's resume and employment paperwork before heading out for the day. Better to be safe than sorry.

※

AFTER DILLON KISSED HER GOODBYE, Kaitlyn returned to the kitchen. Jack sat at the table staring into the winter wonderland outside. "Mom, can we go play in the snow?"

Kaitlyn sucked in her breath. She didn't want to disappoint him, but she was so far behind on work. She needed to check with Melody and make sure the office was still running and then she had to get to drawing. "I'll tell you what, if you promise to stay right there where I can see you, I'll let you go out by yourself."

His mouth opened and he danced from one foot to the other. "Really?"

Kaitlyn laughed at his reaction, but she couldn't really blame him. She was overprotective and she rarely let him outside alone unless it was in their backyard which was fully fenced in. Part of her fear was a stranger taking him, but a bigger part was a worry that Jerry might come back. He hadn't fought the divorce, but Kaitlyn still lived in fear that one day he would return and assert parental rights. "Yes, really. Let's go get you dressed warmly, and then you can go outside. I'll sit right here and work on my sketching so I can see you."

"Okay." He scurried to the stairs and half jumped, half skipped to the top and down the hallway to their room where he stood impatiently waiting for her. "Come on, Mom, hurry up."

"I'm coming." She inserted the key and opened the door. While he added extra layers, she grabbed some pencils and her sketchpad from her work bag. She hadn't known she would be sketching here, but she always carried it with her in case inspiration struck.

When she was sure Jack was toasty, they headed back to the kitchen and she opened the sliding glass door for him. Her heart tightened as he skipped outside, and a tiny inkling of fear crept in. Was she doing the right thing? Maybe she could put off work and go outside with him. What if something happened to him?

"I used to let Dillon play alone outside all the time as a boy," Margie said from behind her.

Kaitlyn turned. "Am I that obvious?"

Margie smiled. "It doesn't get any easier as they get older either. I worried every time Dillon was away from me, but at some point, you do have to let them fly a little."

A large sigh escaped Kaitlyn's lips. "I suppose." She spared one more look at Jack before returning to the table and sitting back down. "I think it's harder because he has no father figure, and I'm afraid he might follow some man off just to know what he's missing."

Margie sat across from her. "Can I ask what happened to his father?"

Kaitlyn snorted and rolled her eyes. "Is it awful that I don't know and I'm not sure I care?"

"Not necessarily. I guess it wasn't a good marriage then?"

"No, I thought it was, but soon after we got married, Jerry began getting angry. I don't know if it was me, him, or being tied down, but he changed. When I got pregnant, he began to get physical, and I knew I couldn't stay. I filed for divorce shortly after Jack was born and for some reason, Jerry didn't fight it. He's never had a father figure."

"I know boys need good men in their lives, but I think you're doing a pretty good job. And I have no doubt that God will send you the right man. Now, I know I'm biased but I happen to think Dillon might be that man, but even if he's not, I know God will provide."

Margie's words warmed Kaitlyn's heart. She had never had the highest self-esteem and it had been rocked after Jerry, but it was starting to build back up. "Thank you, Margie. I'm glad we reconnected. I've missed these talks."

Margie patted her hand. "Me too, my dear. I always considered you like a daughter." She leaned forward a little. "Maybe one day you really will be."

Heat flared across Kaitlyn's face, but she returned the smile. "Maybe one day I will."

"Well, I'll let you get to work. I'm hoping that sketch pad means you are working on ideas for my guest rooms?"

"Absolutely. I'll have to go back to Denver for a week or so, but then I can come back and begin work if that's okay with you."

"I would love that." Margie flashed one final smile before exiting the room.

Kaitlyn glanced one more time outside, but Jack was playing happily in the snow. He threw up a handful of snow and danced underneath it. Okay, he was all right. She could get to work now. Kaitlyn opened her sketchbook and closed her eyes as she tried to envision how the guest rooms should look. When she had a picture in her head, she snapped her eyes open and began sketching the designs out.

As often happened when she was working, Kaitlyn got lost in her work. Until her phone rang. She glanced at the caller ID. Melody. Oh good, she needed to talk to her and had meant to call her earlier.

"Hey, Melody, how was your Christmas?"

"It was good. How was yours?"

"Busy, but also good. At least until Dillon's ex girlfriend showed up."

"What?" Even across the phone, the shock was evident in Melody's voice. "I totally thought he was into you."

"He is or at least I'm pretty sure he is. We're even talking about getting back together and having dinner tonight."

"I don't understand. Boy, I missed a lot."

Kaitlyn smiled. "Yeah, I guess you did." She glanced to the backyard to check on Jack and her hand gripped the phone tighter. Jack was nowhere to be found.

"So.... spill. I want to hear all about it."

"Uh, hang on." Kaitlyn stood and walked to the glass door. Her eyes scanned left and right, but there was no sign of Jack. "Melody, can I call you right back? I have to find my son."

"Sure, is everything okay?" Melody's voice had shifted from fun and flirty to worried.

"I'm not sure. He was supposed to be playing outside, but I got busy drawing and now he's gone." Worry didn't even begin to describe the feeling squeezing Kaitlyn's heart right now. Fear choked her lungs and each breath became an issue.

"Don't worry, I'm sure he's just around the side. Go check, and call me after."

"I will." Kaitlyn ended the call and shoved it in her pocket. Without even grabbing her coat, Kaitlyn flung open the door and charged into the snowy backyard. "Jack?" Her voice trembled with emotion. "Jack?"

She looked to the right but he wasn't there either. The left side jutted out a little more, so she hurried to the end of it and looked left. Nothing but white stillness. "Jack?" Desperation filled her voice as she screamed at the top of her lungs. "Jack."

"What, Mom?"

She whirled around to find Jack and Julian behind her. They had either come from the forest when her back was turned or from the side of the building behind her.

"Where were you? You were supposed to stay where I

could see you." Kaitlyn cringed at the coldness in her voice, but she had been so worried. Her emotions were still rattling out of control inside her.

"Sorry, Mommy, but Julian wanted to show me this really cool tree. It kind of bends toward the ground instead of up. He says in the summer it's a great climbing tree."

"That's great, but Julian," she fixed him with an icy stare, "should have asked your mother if he could take you somewhere first."

A look of chagrin crossed Julian's features. "You're right, and I'm sorry. You just looked so focused in there that I didn't want to interrupt your work."

Kaitlyn almost believed he was sorry. His words were right, his tone was right, but there was still something in his eyes that didn't sit well with her. "It's fine, but it's past lunch time, and I think it's time Jack came inside."

"Ah, Mom, do I have to?"

"Yes, you have to. Maybe you can come out later….. With Margie if she's available." Kaitlyn made sure to look at Julian when she said 'with Margie.' She didn't want to poke the bear as she had no idea what he might do, but she wanted him to be aware that she was not pleased.

Jack's small shoulders rose and fell with his sigh. "All right. Thanks again, Julian. The tree was cool."

"No problem, little man." Though his words were said to Jack, his eyes never left Kaitlyn's, and she suppressed the shudder that wanted to race through her body.

Suddenly, she felt the cold. It curled around her with sharp talons and burned her skin. "Let's go." She grabbed Jack's hand and led him back inside, clenching her jaw to keep it from chattering.

"It was just Julian, Mom. I didn't go with a stranger. I thought it would be okay," Jack said as they crossed the white expanse.

"We'll talk about it inside," Kaitlyn hissed and sped up her steps.

When they were safely back in the house, she shut the door behind her and glanced back. Julian was gone, and she didn't think he was anywhere he could hear her. "Look, buddy, I'm sure Julian is nice, but I don't know him well. I would just like you to have Margie, Dillon, or myself with you wherever you go, okay?"

"Okay," Jack said with a sigh. "Can I go play in our room?"

Kaitlyn closed her eyes and took a deep breath. He was only five. She needed to remember that. What was important to her sometimes went over his head, and she had no concrete reason to tell him to stay away from Julian. It was just a feeling and five year olds didn't always understand feelings. "Yes, you can go play, but remember what I said. Don't go anywhere with Julian without coming and telling me first."

Though she still had work to do, Kaitlyn followed him up

the stairs and made sure he was in the room with the door closed before she returned to the table. She fell into the chair and let herself shake for a moment, releasing the pent up emotions that had been building inside her. Then she pulled out her phone and called Melody back. Her business partner was more like a sister, and Kaitlyn knew she would worry until she heard.

"Did you find him?" Melody had picked up on the second ring.

"Yeah, he was off somewhere with Julian."

"Oh, well that's okay then." Kaitlyn said nothing and the pause stretched out. "Right?"

"I honestly don't know. There's been a few odd incidents and there is just something about him that bugs me, but I can't place my finger on it."

"Wow, I should have come for Christmas. I've missed a lot. Julian's not a good guy, you and Dillon are back together, but his ex is in town. It's like a Christmas Hallmark movie, and I can't believe I'm missing it all."

"Don't forget the cover picture," Kaitlyn said relaxing with Melody's teasing words. "The photographer was something else, and Dillon and I are on the cover together. Actually, Dillon, Jack, and I."

"What? How do you know that?"

"Dillon's ex is a model and I guess she knows the photographer who sent her the cover picture."

"My head is literally spinning over here. This is the most

excitement you've had in …. Pretty much since I've known you."

"Haha," Kaitlyn replied though the statement was true. Not that she was enjoying *all* the excitement, but it certainly had been awhile since she'd had any. "How is the business going? Any new jobs?"

"Oh, right, that's why I called. Evidently, word got out that you were redecorating the lodge. A few other local businesses have called wanting to set up a meeting with us."

"You mean you. I don't generally do businesses. The only reason I'm doing the lodge is because it's more like doing a house. Besides, Margie wants me to redo the guest rooms too."

Melody let out a squeal on the other end of the phone. "That's wonderful. We'll both be busy for the next few weeks then. Oops, gotta run, the other line is ringing." The phone clicked in Kaitlyn's ear and she chuckled. Melody hadn't even said goodbye, but that's just who she was. She had a lot of passion for what she did. Sometimes so much that she forgot common courtesy when something grabbed her attention.

Kaitlyn set the phone on the table to continue sketching, but before she could pick up the pencil, it buzzed and vibrated. Had Melody forgotten to tell her something? She glanced at the screen, but the text message was not from Melody but from Dillon.

"Giada's Italian Kitchen. Six pm."

Kaitlyn glanced at her watch. It was nearing one. That would give her another few hours to finish the designs before she had to shower and dress for the date. After replying she would meet him there, she tucked her phone back in her pocket and returned to her sketches.

Four hours later, she closed the book. The rough sketches were done, and her hand ached. She'd load them into her computer program later. Right now, she needed to move.

Jack was asleep on the bed when she entered the room. He rarely napped anymore, but when he was sick or had played especially hard, he would often crash in the afternoons or early evenings. Kaitlyn was then always stuck with the dilemma of letting him sleep, though he might wake in the middle of the night starving, or waking him up to make sure he ate and take the chance he might not fall back to sleep at his regular bed time.

She decided this time to let him sleep. After her shower, she would find Margie and let her know. Since he hadn't had lunch that she knew of, Kaitlyn was certain his stomach would wake him in the next hour anyway.

Kaitlyn removed her charm bracelet and set it on the sink before taking off her clothes. The gift had been so thoughtful, and though Dillon said she owed him nothing in return, Kaitlyn knew she wouldn't feel right until she had gotten him something equally fitting. She ran through ideas as she stepped into the shower, but none of them seemed right. Kaitlyn supposed she would know it when she saw it.

As Kaitlyn emerged from the bathroom, washed, dried, and dressed, Jack stirred on the bed. His eyes popped open though they didn't quite focus on her. "Where you going, Mommy?"

"To dinner with Dillon. You hungry?"

"Yeah, can we do McDonalds?" The stupor of sleep fled from his body as he bolted upright on the bed.

Kaitlyn chuckled and ruffled his hair. "No, I'm going to dinner. You are staying here, but let's go find Margie. Maybe she'll make you a hamburger for dinner."

"Yay, hamburger." Jack scrambled off the bed and to the door. "Come on, Mom, I'm starving."

They found Margie in the kitchen whipping up some dinner. She looked up as they entered. "Oh, there you are. I was wondering if you might be getting hungry."

"I am." Jack grinned and rubbed his belly. "What are you making?"

"I'm making cheeseburger casserole." She laughed as Jack scrunched up his face. "I know. I thought I didn't like casseroles when I was your age either, but this one is really good. It's like having a cheeseburger only you eat it with a fork."

Jack still didn't look convinced. "Okay, if you say so."

"Just try it," Kaitlyn told him. "You might like it." She

turned her attention to Margie. "Thanks again for watching him. I don't think we'll be out late."

Margie winked at her. "Stay as long as you like. I'm sure I can keep Jack entertained for a while."

Kaitlyn felt another blush steal over her. "Be good for Margie," she said to Jack and gave him a hug. Then she grabbed her coat and opened the front door, excited for the upcoming dinner.

CHAPTER 12

Dillon stared at the paper Dan had handed him. "I don't understand. Are you telling me Julian Davis is not a man in his thirties working for my mother?"

"I don't know who is working for your mother, but his name isn't Julian Davis. This social you gave me is fake, probably so the guy wouldn't have to pay taxes."

Fear coursed through Dillon's veins. Who was this man his mother had hired and what did he want? Worse yet, was his mother safe with him there? Was Kaitlyn? Or had she already arrived in town? "What do I do? Is there anything?"

"I have to pick him up with the knowledge I have. I can't guarantee the penalty will be much though, maybe a year in jail for falsifying his name and social. Of course, if anything else is in his background when we find out who he really is, I promise I'll do my best. Has he done anything else?"

Dillon shook his head. "I think he might have stolen a charm from my room, but I can't prove it."

"Even theft would add a few more years. Let's go pick this guy up, and I'll work on getting a search warrant for his room."

Dillon nodded, but his head was spinning with all the information. How long had Julian been working for his mother? What was his purpose in lying to her? "Yeah, I just need to... what time is it?"

Dan glanced at his wrist. "Three past six."

"What?" Dillon snapped to attention. That meant Kaitlyn was already at the restaurant. He needed to contact her to explain his tardiness. "Give me a second. I'm supposed to be somewhere, and I'm late." He pulled his cell phone out of his pocket and punched in Kaitlyn's number.

"Come on, come on," he muttered as the phone rang. "Pick up."

"Hi, this is Kaitlyn Bell, I can't get to my phone right now..."

"Argh. I can't get her on the phone. She might be in trouble. Can you come with me and then we can pick up Julian?"

"Sure, let me inform the higher ups in case we need backup." Dan stepped into the back office for a minute and then he was back, gun strapped to his side. "Let's go."

As he pushed open the door, Dillon's head tilted.

Something didn't look right with his truck. He took another step closer. "I think we might have more evidence."

Dan whistled as he took in the slashed tires. Not just one, but all four. "That takes some guts to slash tires on a truck while it's parked at a police station."

"Yeah, I think Kaitlyn and my apprehension around him may have caused him to escalate. Any chance I can get a ride?"

Dan smiled and Dillon realized he didn't look much older than he had when Dillon had been a kid. "You bet you can. Let's go get this guy."

KAITLYN CHECKED her phone as she parked. Two minutes to spare. She glanced around the parking lot and was surprised not to see Dillon's truck. What could be taking him so long in town?

She dropped the phone back in her purse; she'd opted for a skirt for dinner and it had no pocket. As she stepped out of the SUV, the hairs on the back of her neck prickled. She had the feeling someone was watching her, but after a survey of the parking lot, she could see no one. Surely she was still just on edge after the incident with Julian earlier.

The snow crunched under her boots as she made her way up the sidewalk and into the restaurant. Inside, the lighting was dim, and Kaitlyn had to blink a few times to make her eyes adjust.

A woman in a crisp white shirt and black pants stood behind a desk near the entrance. "May I help you?" she asked as Kaitlyn approached.

"Yes, I'm supposed to be meeting Dillon Fields here. He said he made a reservation."

The woman dropped her eyes to scan a sheet in front of her. "Here he is. Right this way."

Kaitlyn followed the woman to a table in the far back of the restaurant. "It appears you have arrived first. Would you like to wait or go ahead and sit down?"

"I'll sit. I'm sure he's just running a few minutes late."

The woman flashed a smile, but it was one of those I'm-sure-you're-right-though-that's-never-the-case kind of smiles. Then she handed Kaitlyn one menu and placed the other on the table across from her. "I'll be right back with some water."

Kaitlyn opened the menu and dropped her eyes to scan the offerings. She was a sucker for Italian food, and every-thing sounded delicious. A chair scraped against the floor, and her face shot up to welcome Dillon. But it was not Dillon who sat across from her.

"Julian, what are you doing here?"

A smile spread across his features. "I thought you might be lonely since Dillon won't make it."

Fear covered Kaitlyn, but she tried to stay composed.

She was safe as long as she stayed in the restaurant. "And why is that?"

"He's off with his girlfriend. You know the leggy blond from last night?"

Even though Kaitlyn suspected Julian wasn't telling the truth, a tiny kernel of doubt and jealousy sprouted within her. Dillon would never do that, would he? "And how would you know that?"

"Because I just saw him over at Stetson's, the steak house. They looked pretty cozy to me."

"I see. And how did you know I'd be here?" Kaitlyn's heart was thundering in her chest. She just hoped Julian couldn't hear it.

"Let's not be coy, Kaitlyn. You know I'm interested in you. I overheard you and Dillon talking." He reached across the table for her hand.

She wanted to yank it out of his grip. His hand was hot and clammy, and his touch sent a shudder through her.

"Now, how about we get out of here and go somewhere private?"

"I don't think you'll be going anywhere except to jail." A man in a police uniform clapped his hand down on Julian's shoulder. Dillon appeared behind the man.

"What for? Last time I checked, it's not illegal to have dinner with a friend." Julian's voice was confident, but Kaitlyn saw the flicker of fear cross his eyes.

"That's true, but falsifying your ID is. I'm not sure who

you are, but you're not Julian Davis. Now please stand up and put your hands behind your back." He hauled Julian to his feet and snapped handcuffs on his wrists. "You have the right to remain silent," he began as he walked Julian towards the entrance.

Dillon watched them for a minute before he turned back to Kaitlyn. A sheepish smile was on his face. "Sorry, I'm late."

Relief flooded Kaitlyn and she sagged back in her chair. "You are forgiven. I don't want to think about what would have happened if you hadn't shown up."

"Me either." Dillon sat down in the seat recently vacated and grasped Kaitlyn's hand.

"Who do you think he is?" Kaitlyn glanced back toward the entrance afraid that somehow he would have escaped the police escort and come back for her.

"I don't know, but Dan will find out. I'm glad I went to see him today."

"Me too." Kaitlyn bit her lip. She didn't want to second guess Dillon, and she was sure Julian had been lying, but she had to know. "Can I ask why you were in town today?"

"Oh, yeah, I almost forgot." He reached into his pocket and pulled out a box. "I came into town for this. I had purchased it earlier, but somehow it disappeared. I'm pretty sure we'll find it in Julian's room."

Kaitlyn took the box and opened it. Her breath caught in her throat as she looked at the charm. It was a tiny representation of a boy and a girl at a movie theater. Their first official date. As if just yesterday, the memory played in her mind.

Kaitlyn stood in her living room waiting for the knock. She'd started getting ready almost an hour ago to make sure she was perfect when Dillon arrived. Dillon Fields. She still couldn't believe he had asked her out. Dillon was the star quarterback and she was…. She was the shy art student. Yet, he had sought her out after her mother died and friended her. Their friendship had grown over the years, and though Kaitlyn harbored feelings for him, she hadn't though they were returned. Until now.

"Where are you guys going again?" her father asked from his chair. He had gotten home early enough to have dinner with her tonight - a rarity. She knew he needed to work, especially with her mother gone, but Kaitlyn sure wished he could be home more often.

"Just to the movies, Dad. We'll probably only be gone for two to three hours."

His eyes traveled down to her toes, and his eyebrow arched. "You're a little dressed up for a movie, aren't you?"

Heat spread across Kaitlyn's cheeks. She had picked a cute skirt and top to wear to the movies. Jeans just didn't seem right for a first date. The knock on the door saved her from having to answer, and she hurried to open the door.

"Wow!" Dillon blinked at her. "You look beautiful."

The heat which had just started receding, flared again. *"Thank you."*

"Hello, Mr. Bell," Dillon said, addressing her father.

"Hello, Dillon. I assume I don't have to give you the speech about Kaitlyn being my daughter and you being on your best behavior."

Kaitlyn looked down at the floor, mortified. "Dad," she muttered.

This time the red spread across Dillon's cheeks. "No, sir. I have nothing but the best intentions toward your daughter."

"Good to hear. You two have fun."

Kaitlyn knew this was their chance to escape before her father said anything else and embarrassed them both. She grabbed Dillon's hand, shouted a goodbye to her father, and pulled Dillon out the door.

"Sorry about my dad," she said as she pulled the door shut behind her.

"It's fine. I can understand his hesitation. After all, you are his only daughter."

Kaitlyn laughed and shook her head. "I'm his only child."

"Even more reason for him to be protective." They reached the car, but before he opened her door, he turned her to face him. "I don't want to ever hurt you, Kaitlyn."

Kaitlyn's heart sped up in her chest. He was so close she could see the tiny gold flecks in his brown eyes. She wanted to reach up and touch his face, but her body felt frozen. How many times had she imagined this moment? It was as if time stood still. His hand grazed her cheek as he tucked a strand of hair behind her ear. Then he curled his hand around the back of her neck. Could he hear her heart hammering in her chest?

It seemed like an eternity as he stared into her eyes, her soul, but finally, his eyes closed, and Kaitlyn knew the moment was finally here. She shut her eyes, so she could focus on her other senses. The feel of his lips, the taste. They were soft like satin when they touched hers. Not hot, but a flame erupted within her nonetheless. The kiss lasted only a moment, but the tingling sensation stayed much longer.

"We better get going or we'll miss the movie," he said as he pulled back.

She could only nod. Her throat seemed unwilling to speak.

He flashed a crooked smile at her and opened her door. Kaitlyn climbed in, and as Dillon walked around to the driver's side door, she touched her lips. They weren't hot to the touch, but the fire inside her hadn't cooled. If this was what kissing was like, she hoped they shared many more in the future.

"It's beautiful, Dillon."

"It's nowhere near as beautiful as you."

Kaitlyn smiled. She wanted to enjoy the moment, but she

had one nagging doubt that she had to clear up first. "So, you didn't see Shana today?"

Dillon's forehead creased. "No, why would I see Shana?"

"I'm sorry. I knew it wasn't true, but when you were late, Julian said he saw you with Shana. I just had to ask."

"It's okay. I understand your concern with Shana, but I promise you, she is out of my life. I only have room in my heart for one woman and that woman is you."

With those words, all the stress and doubt from before shattered, and Kaitlyn felt relief for the first time in days. Now, they could talk about the bigger issue at hand. "Does your mother know about Julian?"

Dillon shook his head. "No, I told her I was going to check him out today, but I haven't had a chance to talk to her. She's going to be so disappointed."

"I just don't get it. Why pretend to be someone else?"

Dillon shook his head, but before he could speak, the waitress appeared at their table. "Sorry, I was told to give you some time after the incident. Are the two of you okay?"

"We are," Dillon said. "Can we get a bottle of your best wine? I believe we'd like to celebrate."

The waitress smiled. "Absolutely. I'll be right back with it."

As she turned away, Kaitlyn glanced back down at the menu. In all the commotion, she had almost forgotten they were there for dinner.

"Do you know what you want?" Dillon asked as he perused his own menu.

Kaitlyn chuckled. "I thought I felt like spaghetti, but now I'm feeling more like the sampler platter."

"Living on the edge, huh?"

"I guess so." She smiled at Dillon as the waitress returned with their glasses and they placed their order.

Though their conversation drifted away from Julian, Kaitlyn couldn't get him out of her mind. Who was he really? And why was there something about him that seemed familiar?

When dinner ended, Dillon picked up the check and took Kaitlyn's hand as they left the restaurant. "I hope you don't mind giving me a ride back."

"Of course not," she said, "but why? What happened to your truck?"

"Someone slashed my tires while I was parked at the police station."

"Julian?"

"I can't think of anyone else. He must really have wanted to get you alone."

Those words sent a shiver down Kaitlyn's spine. Had Dillon been somewhere more remote, she might not have been rescued and who knows what would have happened. As she climbed in the driver's side, she thanked God for watching out for her and for sending Dillon back into her life. She didn't know how they were going to work out the distance or what the future might hold, but she was sure she wanted Dillon in it.

DILLON HOPED his mother would have gone to bed before they arrived back at the lodge, so he could have some time to figure out how to tell her about Julian, but it was not to be. As soon as they opened the front door, they found her and Jack on the couch watching a Christmas movie.

"How was dinner?" his mother asked as they approached.

"Dinner was good," Kaitlyn said. She squeezed Dillon's hand. "We can talk more about it in a minute, but I need to get this little man to bed real quick."

"Aw, Mom, can't I finish the movie?"

"No, we'll finish it tomorrow. Dillon and I need to talk to Margie."

Jack sighed, but he rose from the couch and followed Kaitlyn to her room. Dillon waited until they were out of the room before sitting next to his mother.

"Why do I have the feeling I'm not going to like this?" his mother asked.

Dillon took a deep breath. "I went to see Dan today. He ran the name Julian Davis through the database, but he doesn't exist. Julian used a fake social, Mom."

"So, who is he?"

"We don't know yet. Dan picked him up and took him in. They'll run his fingerprints through the system and let us know if anything shows up. Also, the police will probably come in the next few days with a warrant for his room."

His mother's eyes widened. "Oh dear, I was hoping to keep this from the guests if at all possible."

"I'll talk to Dan. Maybe he can just have a few people in plain clothes come in to gather what they need. His room is in the caretaker apartment, isn't it?" The lodge had a small attached building that held an apartment for the groundskeeper. Because that position was year round, it was a benefit offered to keep him or her from having to drive everyday.

"Yes, I suppose that does help. They could enter from the back that way."

Dillon took her hand. "I'm really sorry, Mom. I wish I could have been wrong."

"Me too, but I'm more glad that no one was hurt. I shudder to think about how long he was here and what he could have done to me or the other guests."

"Yes, we got lucky. Unfortunately, I can't say the same for my truck. He slashed all my tires."

Her hand flew to her mouth. "Oh no, I'll help pay for the damage."

"It's fine, Mother. My more immediate concern is getting you a new groundskeeper. I will help out until that time, but it certainly isn't my specialty."

"I'm sure it will be fine. I just wish your father were still here."

"Me too, Mom. Me too."

KAITLYN WOKE the next morning relieved and sad. She was glad Julian had been taken care of and wouldn't be around, but she was sad that they'd be leaving today as well. It had been nice to get away from work for a bit and return to a simpler time. However, it was time to return to work, and she was sure her father would want to come around soon and celebrate Christmas with Jack. Plus, she had so much to tell Melody.

Jack roused as she finished dressing. "You ready for breakfast, kiddo?"

He rubbed his eyes and stretched. "Do we have to go home today?"

"Yeah, I'm afraid so, but we can come back."

"All right. I guess I do miss my room and my stuffed animals."

Kaitlyn bit back a smile. Oh, to be five again.

After Jack dressed, they headed downstairs where the sweet smell of sugar and cinnamon greeted them. Kaitlyn could almost feel her stomach growing. She would have to get back into her gym routine when she returned home. Her pants were fitting just a little too snugly lately.

Margie stood at the island icing an enormous pan of cinnamon rolls. "Well, good morning. I thought since you guys would be leaving today, you could use some hearty cinnamon rolls for the drive back."

"Yay, I love cinnamon rolls," Jack said. "Momma never makes them."

"Momma rarely has time as she's usually herding you out the door to get you to the nanny and myself to work on time." Still, Kaitlyn made a mental note to try and cook breakfast more often. While she often cooked for herself, it was easier to snag a pop tart or a frozen waffle for Jack and let him eat it on the way.

"I thought I smelled cinnamon rolls," Dillon said as he entered the room. "Thanks, Mom." He planted a kiss on Margie's cheek and flashed a wink at Kaitlyn before grabbing a mug to fill with coffee.

Kaitlyn grabbed one as well and filled a glass of milk for Jack. Then they took their seats around the table. They had just finished breakfast when the chime announced someone entering the front door.

"Duty calls," Margie said standing, "I'll be right back."

As she headed to the living room to greet the guest, Kaitlyn grabbed hers and Jack's plate and took them to the sink.

"Dillon, Kaitlyn, I've got some news." Kaitlyn turned to see the man from the night before standing in the doorway.

"Jack, why don't you go play your tablet for bit?"

Jack looked from one adult to the next and must have decided by their serious expressions that he didn't need to stay because he bounded out of the room.

"So, I informed Dillon yesterday that Julian Davis was not his real name. However, we had no idea who he was. When I arrested him yesterday, we ran his fingerprints. His actual name is Barry Glendale."

Barry Glendale? Why did that name seem familiar to her? Kaitlyn placed the rinsed plates in the sink and returned to the table. "Did he say why he did it?"

The officer shook his head. "No, I'm afraid he isn't saying much. We'll keep working, but does that name sound familiar to any of you? Can you think of any reason why he might target you?"

Dillon and Margie shook their heads, but Kaitlyn closed her eyes and tried to focus on the elusive element. She'd felt something was familiar about Julian and the name sounded even more familiar. Suddenly it hit her. "Dillon, do you have an old yearbook around here?"

"A yearbook? I don't know." He looked to Margie. "Did we keep any of them?"

"I kept all of them. You never know when you might want to look through them again. They're in the sunroom in one of the boxes."

Kaitlyn groaned inwardly. None of those boxes were labeled. However, she had gone through most of them looking for the Christmas decorations so at least the job would be shorter now.

"You think this is someone we went to school with?" Dillon asked.

"Maybe. There was something in the way Julian er Barry looked at me that seemed familiar and the name...I just feel like I've heard it before. I think he might have even been in our class, but I want to be sure before we send this nice officer on a goose chase."

"Dan, you can call me Dan," the officer said.

"Why don't you two go look and I'll get Dan some breakfast?" Margie said as she scooped out a few rolls and placed them on a plate.

Kaitlyn paused for just a moment as the look Margie had flashed Dan registered in her brain. Was Margie interested in this man? She'd have to follow up later. "Come on, Dillon."

She grabbed his hand and pulled him down the hall to the sun room. "Okay, I've already gone through all those boxes." She pointed to the first three rows. "So, that just leaves those two."

"All right, let's get to it." Dillon grabbed one box and Kaitlyn another. They sat on the floor and opened the lids.

Kaitlyn's box held tons of papers. All of them appeared to be Dillon's from high school. Assignments, rewards, projects. She'd had no idea Margie was such a pack rat. At least she kept the clutter in boxes though. "Hey, do you have a Sharpie?"

"Not on me. Do you think I just walk around with a Sharpie in my pocket all day?"

Kaitlyn glared at him. "I mean do you know where to get one? We could label these boxes before we put them back up so we don't have to do this again."

Dillon smiled. "Oh, well, you should be more particular with your words. However, I think that is a great idea, milady. I shall go and fetch you a Sharpie immediately."

Kaitlyn rolled her eyes as he left the room, but she had missed his silly sense of humor. She continued rifling through the papers, just to make sure she hadn't missed anything. Nothing felt stiff enough to be a yearbook, but at the bottom of the pile, her fingers touched something odd. She grabbed it and pulled it out, smiling as she recognized it.

It was a note folded like a tiny letter. She and Dillon used to pass them back and forth in the hall when they didn't have class together. While cell phones had existed back then, most plans charged per text sent, so they couldn't communicate through their phones often. Kaitlyn hadn't minded. This way had always seemed more personal anyway. She unfolded the note and read the faded scribble.

Dillon-

How is your day going? Geometry is killing me today. When am I ever going to need to write a proof as a decorator? Oh man, Fred Jones just threw a pencil and got it stuck in the ceiling. Ms. Bailey is mad. I better wrap this up. Can't wait till lunch to see you.

Kaitlyn

"Here is your Sharpie per your request." Dillon bowed and held the marker out to her. "What do you have there?"

"An old note I wrote you." She held it out to him. "Do you remember when we used to drop these in each other's lockers or hand them off in the hallway?"

Dillon chuckled. "I do. Man, am I glad we don't have to do that anymore."

"I don't know. I kind of miss it. Though I guess it wouldn't be practical now." A silence fell as Kaitlyn realized she wouldn't see Dillon every day when she returned home.

As if reading her mind, Dillon stepped forward and grabbed her hand. "Don't worry. We'll figure something out. It's only ninety minutes."

"Yeah, I just realized I was going to miss seeing you everyday."

"Me too." He squeezed her hand and bent down to plant a kiss on her lips. "Now, let's get back to work before my mother proposes to Dan."

Kaitlyn gasped. "You saw that too?"

"Yeah, I shouldn't be surprised. In fact, I'm a little more surprised they haven't gotten together sooner. Dan was always a good friend to my father, and he and Mother seemed to get along as well. It only makes sense."

"And you're okay if they do?"

Dillon shrugged. "I'm nearly thirty. My mom can date whoever she likes. I miss my dad, but I'd rather she not be alone. And at least someone like Dan might keep her from hiring someone like Barry again."

"Speaking of Barry, let's keep looking." Kaitlyn scribbled the words "Dillon's papers" across her box, closed the lid, and replaced it on the shelf. Only four more boxes remained.

"Can you pass me the Sharpie? This one appears to just be photographs."

Kaitlyn handed over the marker and opened the lid of her box. "Dillon." At the top was their yearbook from Senior year and underneath in order was the rest of high school. He joined her as she pulled out the book and flipped to the back. Their high school had been big enough that the yearbook contained a glossary listing each student and the pages they appeared on. Her finger traced down the page until she hit gold. Glendale, Barry page number six, twenty-seven, and fifty-four.

"He wasn't involved in very much if those are the only pages he's listed on," Dillon said reading over her shoulder.

"If he is who I think he is, I remember him being a loner." She flipped to page six but it appeared Barry had missed picture day because the words 'Photo not available' sat in the box where his picture should have been. She flipped over to page twenty-seven which held clubs. Evidently, he had been a member of the chess club, but he was listed as not pictured there as well. On page fifty-four, she struck gold though.

Page fifty-four was a compilation of pictures taken at random moments around the school. A cheerleader at a pep rally, kids working together on a project in a classroom, but it was the bottom one that chilled Kaitlyn's blood. The bottom picture was of Dillon and Kaitlyn eating lunch in the cafeteria, but off to the side was a broody boy with long, shaggy hair who was glaring their direction.

"Hey, I remember that guy. He interviewed me once for the school paper, though I can't remember ever seeing the article."

Kaitlyn shook her head. "That's because he didn't write for the paper, Dillon." She remembered the boy clearly now. He had approached her shortly after she and Dillon began dating exclusively.

"Hello, Kaitlyn."

Kaitlyn closed her locker and turned. A boy she didn't recognize with shaggy hair covering his face stood behind her. "Um, hello." She was at a loss for his name though she was sure she had seen him around.

"Barry. It's Barry, and I've liked you for a long time. I was hoping maybe you'd go to prom with me?"

"Oh, that's very nice of you, Barry, but I already have a date." Dillon hadn't officially asked her, but she assumed since they were going steady that they would be attending prom together.

Barry stiffened and clenched his hands into fists. "With Dillon Fields?" His voice was no longer the shy, quiet voice he had first used, but a cold, emotionless, and flat tone.

"Well, he is my boyfriend." Kaitlyn glanced to the left and right. Though Barry hadn't threatened her, she wanted to make sure people were around in case he escalated.

"Dillon Fields is nothing. Mark my words. One day I will have everything he does and more."

"That's great. I hope you find what you're looking for. I have to run now, but it was nice to meet you, Barry." Kaitlyn hurried off before Barry could say anything else to her.

"He asked me to prom once. I forgot all about it, because you asked me to prom the same night. He told me then that one day he would have everything you did and more."

Dillon stared at her as if he didn't understand. Then his eyes widened. "You think he was trying to become me?"

"It makes sense. He probably kept tabs on the lodge after you left and when a position opened, he swooped in."

Dillon shuddered. "That should make me feel better, knowing the why, but knowing he was watching me for so long is creepy. Especially since I didn't even know it."

"Come on, let's go show Dan."

DAN and his mother were engaged in some deep conversation when they entered the kitchen. Like guilty teenagers, they jumped apart.

"Did you find something?" Dan asked.

"We did." Kaitlyn handed the yearbook over. "I don't know how we didn't notice this picture when we got our yearbook. I remembered him asking me to prom, and when I declined, he told me he would have everything Dillon did one day."

"We think he was trying to become me or at least take over as your son," Dillon said. The words felt like rocks on his tongue as he spoke them. How could he not have known this boy was watching him? Had he been that focused on himself? That answer was obvious. Of course he had. His self-absorption had been the reason he left Kaitlyn. Even back then, he had believed his goals were more important than hers.

"I can't believe I fell for him," Margie said. Her hands shook as she gripped her mug. His mother wasn't much of a coffee drinker, so Dillon assumed it was tea.

Dan's hand covered hers. "It's not your fault. He was very charming, and his documentation appeared real. Only someone used to seeing forgeries would have spotted it."

"I wonder why he chose Dillon though." Kaitlyn squeezed Dillon's hand and offered him a smile.

"It could be as simple as the fact that he was well-known. His family owned this lodge, which people knew about, he was a star football player, and-"

"He was too self absorbed to notice," Dillon finished for him.

"I wasn't going to say that."

"Maybe not, but it's true. I barely even came home for Dad's funeral because it interfered with my project."

"We all get caught up in life, son. No one is blaming you for this, but if it helps you re-evaluate your life, consider that a blessing." He turned to Dillon's mother. "Some of us go too long before doing that and then realize what all we've missed that we could have had."

"Um, am I missing something?"

His mother's face turned pink. "I never told you before because I didn't want you to think something was going on. I loved your father very much, but I met him after I lost the man I thought I was going to marry. Dan and I were high school sweethearts, but we both wanted different things after school. Dan went to the academy, and I stayed here to help my family with the lodge. I met your father shortly after that when he moved to town. We dated, fell in love, and were married."

Dan took over the story. "A few years later, I realized I loved Margie and returned to Keystone only to find her happily married. I wanted no part of breaking up their marriage, and your father was such a good man that we actually became friends. When he died, I stayed away because I still had feelings for Margie, and I didn't want to act improperly. I figured when she was ready, she would seek me out or perhaps God would throw us together again."

"I'm sorry," Kaitlyn spoke up, "are you saying you never married all this time?"

Dan shook his head and smiled. "I knew Margie was the woman for me. No one would ever compare, and it wouldn't have been fair to any other woman."

"That is so romantic."

Romantic was not the word that came to Dillon's mind. Crazy, unheard of, unsettling maybe.

"Anyway, my point to that story is that we all make mistakes. Accept them and learn from them before you lose years."

Dillon could accept that. He had been self-absorbed in high school and the years beyond, but he could change that now. No, he would change that now. With God's help and Kaitlyn by his side, he would become a better man. The man she needed as a husband and Jack needed as a father.

CHAPTER 13

"Oh my gosh, I feel like you've been gone forever." Melody very nearly attacked Kaitlyn as she walked in the office door the next morning.

"I know. I almost forgot what this place looked like." Kaitlyn set her laptop bag down on her desk. "Do we have anything pressing to do today?"

"No, just working on some designs, why?"

"Because I have so much to tell you."

"This sounds like it might need doughnuts and coffee."

Kaitlyn shook her head and groaned. "No. No more sweets. Margie is a great baker, and I had to put on stretchy pants this morning."

"Haha, okay, how about some popcorn?"

"Sure, get some popcorn. I'll check my email and then tell you everything."

"DILLON, you don't have to stay for this," his mother said as the last applicant left. He was helping her interview for the next groundskeeper, but his mind was a million miles away. Or, more specifically, one hundred miles away in Denver. He hadn't been able to stop thinking about Kaitlyn after he said goodbye to her and Jack yesterday afternoon.

"No, it's fine, Mother, I want to help."

"I know you do, but what you should be doing is buying a ring and proposing to that girl." His mother shuffled the papers and tapped them against the table to even them out.

"A ring? Mom, we've only been back together for a few days. I think it might be too early to propose." Though he couldn't deny the thought had been in his head as well.

"You should have proposed to that girl ten years ago. Remember what Dan said? There's no reason to waste any more time."

Dan. That was a topic that had to be addressed before he could focus completely on Kaitlyn. "Are you going to start seeing him?"

His mother tilted her head as she regarded him. "Is it okay with you if I do?"

"I don't have a reason to say no, and I'd never want to

deny you happiness, but it is a little odd. I mean he was always Dad's friend."

"He was, but before that he was my friend. He lives close, and he's willing to come check on me. At least you wouldn't have to worry so much about your old mother."

"Mom, I said I was coming back to help."

"I know you did, and you can, but maybe you're needed more in Denver right now. It's only ninety minutes away. You could come back anytime."

Dillon mulled the information over in his head. He wanted to be there for his mother, but it was no secret his mind and his heart were with Kaitlyn. And he was nearing thirty. He wanted a family and kids of his own. "Are you sure, Mom? Kaitlyn and I could do long distance for a few months until you feel comfortable with the new hire."

"I'm sure. Now, go and get that woman."

Dillon didn't argue any longer. He kissed his mother on the cheek and headed to his room to pack his things. He'd have to get back to Florida soon to take care of the rest of his items, but he could look for an apartment to rent in Denver until then.

"OH MY GOODNESS. So, this guy went to school with the two of you?" Melody had listened with rapt attention to the entire story. Her popcorn was gone as she'd shoveled it in almost mindlessly throughout the story.

"Yeah. We think he was trying to take over Dillon's life. Dan is supposed to keep me informed if there are any new developments in the case. I never like to see someone go to jail, but I have to admit I'm kind of glad he's gone. He seemed so nice at first, but then he grew creepier and creepier - always appearing out of nowhere like he'd been following and listening."

Melody shook her head. "Wow, and to think I was going to try and get his number."

"I'd say you dodged a bullet there."

"I guess, so are you and Dillon together now?"

Kaitlyn's lips pulled into a smile. "We are, but he's staying at the lodge to help his mother, so we'll only be able to see each other on weekends."

"That's probably okay though, at least for a few weeks. We have a lot of work to catch up on."

DILLON PULLED into the parking lot of the jewelry store and took a deep breath. Had he really been doing this same thing a few weeks ago? It felt so different this time. There wasn't the squeezing on his heart or the difficulty breathing. This time, only the hope he would find the right ring existed.

The jewelry store was brightly lit as he pulled open the

door. Glass cases lined the walls, and two salesmen in dress shirts and ties stood behind them.

"Welcome to Miner's Jewels, how can we help you?" The older gentleman with graying hair and kind eyes smiled at him.

Dillon crossed the space between them. "I'm looking for an engagement ring."

The man smiled. "Those are always my favorite words. Come with me." He walked to the right to the largest case in the room. Dillon followed. This was where his indecision had happened last time, but as he looked over the rings in this case, clarity fell on him. He knew Kaitlyn wouldn't like oval diamonds, so those were out. She went more for the princess cut or the round diamonds. As far as size, he knew she would want at least half a carat but no more than a full carat.

"May I see that one please?" He pointed to a beautiful princess cut ring that sat in the middle of the case. The diamond sat in between two bands. A gold one with small baguettes circled from above the stone and to the left. It angled down to the right making up the side of the ring. At the bottom, it morphed into a silver band that then came up the left side of the ring. It snaked under the diamond and also held baguettes. The diamond seemed to float in the middle of the two colored bands. It was perfect. Beautiful and original. Just like Kaitlyn.

"That is a beautiful choice," the man said as Dillon

examined the ring closer. "It has both gold and silver for the woman who wears both."

Dillon's hand grew warm as he held the ring, and he knew this was probably the one. Still, he scanned the case one more time. He wanted to be absolutely sure, but none of the other rings called to him as this one had. "I'll take this one. I need a size seven."

"This must be your lucky day," the salesman said with a smile. "That ring is already a size seven."

Dillon didn't believe in luck, but he did believe in God. The easiest path wasn't always the right one, but Dillon had learned that when it opened up and everything went right, it probably was a good choice. "Then wrap it up for me."

With the ring tucked in his pocket, Dillon returned to his truck and began the long drive to Denver.

"Hey, Dad, I'm so glad you could make it," Kaitlyn said as she opened the door for her father. He lived about an hour away, but she had called him earlier to let him know she and Jack were back in town, and he had insisted on driving out to do their Christmas celebration.

"I'm glad you're back in town. I was beginning to wonder if I'd ever get to give my grandson his gifts." He held a few packages in each arm.

Kaitlyn swatted his arm as she pulled him inside and shut the door behind him. "We weren't gone that long, Dad."

"Long enough for your tree to start wilting." He walked to the large, pine tree and placed the packages underneath it.

It was true that it had lost many of its needles, but the lights still shone and the ornaments still hung. Though the room wasn't as Christmassy as she had decorated the lodge, Kaitlyn felt the room still held its Christmas cheer.

"Okay, so the tree lost a little water. It has to be recycled soon anyway."

"That is true. I'm still glad to have you back." He crossed back to her and pulled her in for a hug. "Now where is my grandson?"

"Probably in his room playing on his tablet. Blessing and a curse that thing." Kaitlyn had resisted buying him a tablet because she didn't like the effect technology had on people. Adults everywhere were more focused on their phones than each other, and she was seeing it filter down into children too. However, she'd caved due to this recent trip. Knowing she would need time to work, she'd gotten him one before they left for Keystone to make sure he had a way to keep himself entertained.

"Well, go tell him it's time for presents. I'll just get myself some coffee."

Kaitlyn smiled and shook her head at her father. As long as she could remember, the man drank a pot of coffee a day.

Half in the morning before work and half in the evening after work. It was a wonder the man ever slept.

Jack was indeed on his bed playing his tablet when she pushed open the door. "Look, Mom, it's Thomas. I can race him."

Apps were another thing she hated. The first download was free, but Jack could only do so much before he needed to buy the additional items. Kaitlyn had already erased a few of those games that he had bugged her to spend money on.

"That's wonderful, honey. Think you could put it down for now? Grandpa is here and wants to open Christmas presents with us."

"Yes, presents. I've been waiting all day to open them." He tossed his tablet on his bed and hurried past her out of the room.

All day was a slight exaggeration, but he had asked to open them last night when they returned home, this morning before she dropped him off at the nanny's, and this afternoon as soon as she picked him up.

"Well, there he is," her father said, scooping Jack up as he ran into the room. "I was wondering if I was going to have to return your gift."

"No way. I don't care what it is, Grandpa, I want it."

Her father laughed as he set Jack down. "I thought you might. Can you read enough to hand each person their gift?"

Jack puffed out his chest. "I can read my name and

Mommy's. I might not know how to read yours, but you would just get the gifts with the names I can't read."

Her father chuckled again. "That does seem like pretty sound logic. Well, why don't you go get us each one to start with?"

As Jack hurried to the tree, Kaitlyn sat next to her father. A moment later, Jack shoved a package in her hand. "That says you, right?"

Kaitlyn glanced at the tag and smiled at her son. "Yes, it does. Good job." She held the gift on her lap until her father and Jack each had a gift as well. Then they all opened their gift. Kaitlyn received a beautiful sweater, her father a new tie, and Jack a toy shop. Then Jack hurried back to the tree to get more gifts. Kaitlyn wished the opening of presents took a little longer, but with only three of them, it was a speedy process. One day, she hoped to have a much larger family gathering, so they could enjoy the process longer.

When the last gift was opened and the thank yous said, she began picking up the paper and bows to throw away. She had just wadded it all into a ball when the doorbell rang. Who in the world would be ringing her bell at eight pm at night? Even though she knew he was in jail, her first thought, or rather fear, was that Barry had somehow escaped the police, followed her home, and was now prowling around her house.

She shook her head to clear the image and opened the front door. Though not her worst fear, it was still not an image she had expected to see. "Dillon? What are you doing here?"

"I'm moving here," he said with a smile.

Kaitlyn tilted her head. Had she missed something? She thought he understood she wouldn't live with him unless they were married. "Dillon, I-"

He laughed. "No, not in here. Here to Denver. I realized I didn't want to be an hour and a half away from you, and with my mom and Dan getting together, she assured me she had someone to look out for her. So, I packed up my things, drove up here, found an apartment, and started the paperwork. I'll have to stay at a hotel for a few days, but I'm okay with that if it means I get to be close to you and Jack."

As if summoned, Jack appeared behind Kaitlyn. "Hey, Dillon, want to come see all the toys I got?"

Dillon smiled down at him. "I do though I was hoping I would make it in time to participate."

Jack wrinkled his brow. "I don't see any presents. Are they in your truck?"

"No, I just brought one present, but it's for both you and your mom. Oh hey, Frank, good to see you," he said noticing her father on the couch.

Her father stood and extended his hand. "Dillon, nice to see you as well."

"So, you're really moving to Denver?" Kaitlyn asked. Her head was still spinning from the news.

"Yes, I'll have to fly back to Florida in the next week to

take care of things on that end, but I'm ready to start my life here."

He was really moving to be close to her? She had hoped he would someday because her business was here, and she didn't want to pack up and start over. Especially not now that business was growing - Melody had landed two new jobs and Kaitlyn still had all the rooms at the lodge to finish. So, though she was overjoyed, she hadn't expected it to happen so soon.

"You're going to be close by?" Jack asked. "Does that mean we can't go to the lodge anymore?"

Kaitlyn laughed. "Don't worry, buddy, you'll get lots more time at the lodge."

"After you finish re-decorating the rooms, do you think you could do something outside?" Dillon asked turning his attention to her.

"I don't know. I don't usually do outside jobs. That might be more Melody's strength. Why?"

"Well, it's such a lovely place and large enough that I was thinking it would be a good spot for an outdoor wedding. Maybe if we added a gazebo."

Kaitlyn blinked. A gazebo? Had he hit his head? She didn't construct gazebos though she supposed her team could build one. "I suppose, but that really isn't what I do."

"Oh, well, I was rather hoping our wedding could be the first one there." He pulled a box out of his pocket and dropped to one knee.

Was he proposing? Was she ready for marriage?

"Kaitlyn Grace Bell, will you marry me and do me the honor of becoming my wife?" He popped open the lid to the box displaying a beautiful diamond ring.

"Does that mean you're going to be my new dad?" Jack asked as he stared at the ring.

"If your mother will have me." Jack's eyes were focused on hers.

"Please, Mom? Dillon would be a great dad."

"I know my opinion doesn't matter in the grand scheme of things," her father said, "but I happen to agree with Jack. I've been waiting a long time to see you married, and I think your mother would agree you two belong together."

Her mother! Kaitlyn wished her mother were still here so she could be in on this moment, but she knew her mother was watching from Heaven. The proposal felt fast, and yet she had imagined and wished for this moment for over a decade. Somewhere she probably still had a notebook with the words 'Mrs. Kaitlyn Fields' scribbled inside it, and she didn't feel scared. When she had agreed to marry Jerry, she'd been plagued with doubts and her throat had dried up at the thought, but she'd been too scared to say no. She felt none of that now. Kaitlyn felt nothing but pure joy.

"Yes," she said as tears flooded her eyes. "Yes, I will marry you."

Dillon slid the ring onto her finger. Then he picked her

up and twirled her around. "Thank you for making me the happiest man in the world," he whispered into her ear.

As he lowered her to the ground and she wrapped her arms around his neck, she wasn't sure which of them was happier.

CHAPTER 14

"Oh my gosh, what is on your hand?"

As usual, Melody's hawk eyes had caught the ring on Kaitlyn's finger the minute she stepped into the office. Of course, Kaitlyn had probably been drawing attention to the ring as well. She hadn't been able to stop looking at it since last night. It had stayed on her finger through the night and only come off during the shower. Even then, she'd been constantly worried it would get knocked off the counter and into the sink or get lost on the floor. It had been less than twelve hours, but her finger now felt naked without the ring on it.

"It's an engagement ring." Kaitlyn held her hand out so Melody could get a closer look. "Dillon proposed last night."

"What? How? I thought he was still in Keystone."

"He decided to move to Denver. He's finalizing a lease on an apartment today."

Melody blinked and shook her head. "Wow, this has been a crazy two weeks. You went from hating Dillon-"

"I didn't hate him," Kaitlyn interrupted. "I hated that he left, and I think my anger at him was masking my real feelings."

"Whatever." Melody waved a hand to dismiss the notion. "You went from not wanting to be in the room with him to agreeing to marry him. You do know you'll have to be in the room with him a lot now, right?"

Kaitlyn's cheeks ached as she smiled for the thousandth time. It was a habit that had started up again in the last week, and there didn't seem to be an end in sight. "I know. I'm looking forward to that part."

"And what does Jack think?" Melody knew that most of Kaitlyn's dates fizzled because she couldn't imagine the man being a father to Jack.

"He's so excited. He gave Dillon the biggest hug, and when I put him to bed, he asked me how soon Dillon could adopt him."

"Wow! Well, that is exciting news indeed. I feel like I need to attach a camera to you because I keep missing all the good moments."

"Not all of them. You're here for this one." Kaitlyn knew Melody probably expected it, but she was still excited to ask. "Will you be my maid of honor?"

This time it was Melody's turn to grin. "Of course I will. Oh, now I'm excited. Have you set a date yet?"

"No, he just proposed last night. He still has to take care of his place in Florida and settle in before we set a date. However, he did want an outdoor wedding, so I'm hoping he's thinking this summer."

Melody sighed. "An outdoor wedding. That's so romantic. When am I going to find my Prince Charming?"

"Don't worry. I'm sure God will send him soon."

Before Melody could respond, Kaitlyn's phone rang. "Hello, Kaitlyn Bell designs. How can I help you?"

"Kaitlyn? This is Officer Palazzo." He paused as if expecting her to say something, but Kaitlyn wasn't sure who Officer Palazzo was. "From Keystone," he continued and then Kaitlyn made the connection.

"Oh, yes, I'm sorry, Dillon always called you Dan."

"Understandable. Anyway, we finally got the search warrant for Barry's room. Were you missing anything from your luggage or your room?"

"I don't think so. I had lost my locket, but Julian er Barry found it and returned it." Suddenly, a sick feeling covered her. "Why?"

"He had quite the stash of items in his room. Jewelry to underwear. I'll send some pictures over. Can you look at them and let me know if any of the items are yours?"

"Of course I will. Officer Palazzo, he's not getting out any time soon, is he?"

"No, Kaitlyn, he's going away for a time. In addition to the stolen items, we found psychotic ramblings of how he planned to kill Dillon if he ever returned and how he planned to win you over. He may not go to jail, probably a psych ward, but I promise he won't be getting out for a while. If he does get released from the mental institution, he'll still have to serve his jail time for theft."

Those words should make Kaitlyn feel better especially after hearing about the death threat against Dillon, but she felt more sad than anything. What had happened to him to cause this break?

"Thank you, Officer Palazzo."

"What was that about?" Melody asked as Kaitlyn hung up the phone.

"Barry. They searched his room and found a ton of stolen items. Officer Palazzo is going to send over some pictures to see if any of them were mine."

"Ugh, so sorry. I know how that feels. My car was broken into once and it felt like such a violation." Melody shuddered as she uttered the words.

"Well, enough about Barry. I want to show you my designs for the rooms I'm doing for Margie before I show her the final product."

Melody's eyes lit up. "Yes, I can't wait to see them. After I saw that Sunshine Room picture you sent me, I was hoping she would let you redo the whole lodge."

"Me too." The girls shared a smile and headed to Kaitlyn's office.

DILLON SIGNED the lease and shook hands with the agent. "Thank you for making this happen so quickly."

"Absolutely, I'm just glad we had a unit available for you."

"Me too. At least I can cross one thing off my list." Of course he still needed to get a job, take care of his place in Florida, and plan a wedding, but at least he'd have a place to stay while he did it.

He waved goodbye to the agent and dropped the apartment keys in his pocket. It was just past five leaving him enough time to grab some dinner and head to Kaitlyn's. He was excited to see her, but she had also asked that he come over so they could look at the pictures Dan had sent together. She didn't want to open the pictures alone, and he couldn't really blame her. Reading about people who did creepy things was bad enough but knowing someone who did put a whole new light on it.

Half an hour later, he stood at her door, fast food bags in hand.

"Hey you," she said as she opened the door. Then her nose lifted in the air and she sniffed and closed her eyes. "Did you get Chicken Pad Thai from Mr. Wong's?"

Dillon chuckled, glad that some things never changed. Kaitlyn had a been a fan of Mr. Wong's for as long as he could remember, and he was afraid of what she might do if the place ever went out of business. "Of course. I told you I was getting something good."

"Mmm, I knew accepting your proposal was the right thing to do." She wrapped her arms around his neck and pulled him down for a kiss.

"Well, I'm glad," he said when they parted, "but are you going to let me in anytime soon? Not only is the food getting cold, but we're giving quite a show to your neighbors."

"Eh, let them look. I never do anything interesting," Kaitlyn said, "but I am hungry." She pulled him inside and shut the door behind her. "Why don't you get the food set up while I get Jack?"

"You bet." He headed to the kitchen placing the bags down on the table before scrounging in the cupboards for bowls, plates, and silverware.

"Is that Chinese food?" Jack asked as he entered the kitchen a moment later.

"Close. It's Thai food. Do you mean to tell me your mother hasn't shared this with you yet?"

"I have so. He just doesn't remember it. In fact, I'm pretty sure I ate this at least twice a week when I was pregnant with him."

"Oh, no, I remember now," Jack said as Dillon slid a plate his way. "I love this food."

Dillon smiled at Kaitlyn. "Like mother, like son."

After dinner, they watched a movie and then Kaitlyn put Jack to bed. Dillon resisted the urge to look at the pictures until she returned, but his curiosity was growing.

"That boy takes forever to go to sleep sometimes," Kaitlyn said with a sigh as she plopped down next to Dillon.

"I'd say that gets better but I remember staying up late until I was in high school."

"You're not giving me hope here." She slugged his arm before snuggling against it.

He shrugged. "Sorry, what can I say? Guess I'm a realist."

Kaitlyn took a deep breath. "Speaking of realism, shall we address the elephant in the room?"

Dillon knew she was referring to the pictures. "Might as well." She snuggled closer as he pulled out his phone and clicked on the first picture from Dan. Rows of jewelry was spread out on the bed. "There's the charm I got you. I knew he had taken it, and while I was in the shower no less."

Kaitlyn shivered next to him. "There's so many pieces. How long has he been doing this?"

"Probably since he started there. I'm surprised more people didn't complain to Mother, but they probably just chalked the missing pieces up to losing them in the packing. Do you see any pieces that are yours?"

Kaitlyn took the phone from him and enlarged the photo.

"No, I don't recognize anything. I guess I should be relieved."

"Well, there's one more pic." Dillon took back the phone and tapped the next picture. This one was of clothing items: socks, gloves, scarves, even a sweater.

Kaitlyn sucked in her breath. "He took clothes too? I don't know why but that feels worse. More personal or something."

"I agree." He scanned the picture. "I'm pretty sure that's my sock. I thought I had just misplaced it in my packing."

Kaitlyn leaned in. "That's Jack's hat. I thought he had left it on a snowman. And that's my scarf. Ugh, Melody is right. I just feel violated."

"Do you want the item back? I'll text Dan and let him know. We may not even be able to get them, but do you want them if we can?"

"No, I don't think I do. I can buy a new hat and scarf. Having them back would just be a reminder, and I don't want one."

"Me either, but I can be thankful for one thing."

"What's that?" Kaitlyn asked.

"I think our mutual distrust of Barry drove us together even more. We had something to bond over that allowed us to heal from the past."

Kaitlyn shook her head. "Now, that's not being a realist. That's being an optimist, but I think you might be right."

"I'll be whatever it takes to keep you happy," Dillon said as he pulled Kaitlyn into his lap and placed his lips on hers.

She giggled and snuggled closer to him. "I hope you'll just keep doing that for a very long time."

"Happy to oblige," he said as he kissed her again.

EPILOGUE

Six Months Later

"You look absolutely stunning," Melody said as Kaitlyn stepped in front of the mirror.

Kaitlyn spun and examined the dress from all angles. "You don't think it's too much?" Though she was not generally a lace and frills person, she had always imagined getting married in a white dress with a full skirt. Though she had worn a wedding dress when she married Jerry, he had picked it out for her - a simple sheath that had no extras.

This dress made her feel like Cinderella the way it billowed out around her feet. The neckline was a sweetheart dipping low enough to show off her neckline but not too low, and though the sleeves were long, they were made entirely of lace.

"No, I think it fits you perfectly, and Dillon will too."

Kaitlyn smiled at the thought of seeing Dillon in his tux. Though she had helped pick it out, she hadn't seen the full look, just the jacket. They had chosen colors together, and she had seen the tie and vest he picked, but he had refused to let her see the whole outfit.

"If I can't see the bride, then you can't see the groom," he'd said.

"Is everything else ready? The food? Jack? The minister?"

Melody smiled. "Well, I don't know as I've been in here with you, but I think so. Shall I go check?"

Kaitlyn was just about to answer yes when a knock sounded at the door. Melody opened the door a crack to see who it was, then threw it wide to allow Margie to enter.

"Well, aren't you a sight," Margie said.

Kaitlyn's heart filled with emotion for her about-to-be-mother-in-law. Margie had long held a place in her heart, but the last seven months had been amazing. She and Kaitlyn had had long chats while Dillon took Jack through the forest at the lodge. Then Margie and Dan had watched Jack so Kaitlyn and Dillon could have "date time." It was almost as good as having her own mother back.

"Thanks, Margie." Kaitlyn smoothed the skirt of her dress. Her insides were wound up tight and she didn't know what to do with her hands.

"I thought you might like to know that the caterer arrived and the food looks amazing. Jack is dressed and holding the ring pillow like a pro. The preacher and the photographer are both here and ready, and your father looks very dapper and emotional."

Kaitlyn smiled and wiped the wetness from the corner of her eyes. How Margie could have known those were all her questions were beyond her, but she was so thankful for the wonderful woman. "And Dillon?"

Margie smiled. "Dillon is there waiting, but that's all I'm saying. Now, are you ready?"

Kaitlyn took one final look in the mirror. Her dark hair was pulled up in a simple updo with a few tendrils curling by her face. Her veil was attached with a comb to the updo and flowed down her back, a stream of white. Her dress appeared to be fitting correctly, skimming her slim figure from shoulder to waist. But something was missing. Her eyes widened. "Flowers? Did we forget my bouquet?"

"Relax." Melody appeared behind her and handed her the bouquet of roses and carnations. "We had them sitting over there so we could fix your makeup, remember?"

"Right." Kaitlyn didn't actually remember, but everything in the last two hours felt like a blur anyway. She took one final breath, her shoulders raising with the motion and slowly sinking down. "Then I suppose I'm ready."

Margie leaned in to hug her. "You are so beautiful, and I know your mother would be proud."

Kaitlyn could feel the wetness returning to her eyes. She

needed to get her emotions under control or she'd spend the whole ceremony dabbing her eyes.

"Okay, let's go." Melody led the way out of the guest room - no longer a bright yellow but now a classic cream color - and down the stairs of the lodge.

True to Margie's word, Kaitlyn's father stood at the entrance to the back door tugging at his tie. Jack stood to his side staring down at the pillow as if he were afraid he was going to drop it. Grant, Dillon's friend, stood closest to the closed doors. When he saw the girls approaching, his eyes lit up and a smile fluttered across his face. He and Melody had seemed to hit it off during the rehearsal dinner and Kaitlyn wondered if there might be romance in Melody's future. Next to Grant was Dan who had graciously agreed to serve as an usher as long as he could walk Margie down the aisle.

"Kaitlyn, you look like an angel." The voice came from her father's mouth, but she almost didn't recognize it as it was strangled with emotion.

Jack looked up from his pillow at the words and a toothy grin covered his face. "Wow, Mom, you sure clean up nice." The adults all laughed and a hurt look crossed Jack's face. "That's not the right phrase?"

"It's perfect, honey." Kaitlyn kissed the top of his head thankful not only for him but his ability to soften the emotional moment.

"Okay, good. Do you see how careful I'm being with the pillow? I haven't dropped the ring yet."

Kaitlyn bit her lip to keep from laughing. He was so sincere that she didn't have the heart to tell him the ring was tied onto the pillow. "That's wonderful, Jack. You are doing a great job."

She looked to her father who was sniffing discreetly and dabbing at his eyes. "Dad, it's going to be fine. You did this once before, remember?"

"Yeah, but I never liked that guy." He chuckled before sobering up and sniffing one more time. "I'm just thinking about how much like your mother you look and how much she would have loved seeing you marry Dillon."

"Thanks, Dad." Before Kaitlyn could become a weeping mess again, the music started.

Grant turned to the group, hand on the door handle. "Well, here we go. Everyone ready?"

Slight nods and smiles circled the group and Dan and Margie linked arms. Grant opened the door for them and they proceeded down the aisle. Jack went next walking at the slowest pace Kaitlyn had ever seen, still terrified to drop the ring. A titter of laughter trickled through the crowd. Grant and Melody linked arms and followed Jack.

Then the music changed and with a deep breath, Kaitlyn slipped her arm in her father's and began her walk up the aisle.

Dillon's eyes were drawn to Kaitlyn from the moment he saw the back doors of the lodge open. Like an angel on earth, she was a vision of white. Her pale skin was just a few shades darker than her dress which made her dark hair stand out even more. He loved that dark hair. It generally cascaded to her shoulders like ripples of chocolate, but today it was pulled atop her head. Tiny tendrils that he longed to touch framed her face.

She found his eyes as the music changed and she began her walk up the aisle. Though he was sure the audience stood, the surrounding people and noise seemed to fade away. It was just the music and Kaitlyn.

Ten years. He still kicked himself that he had wasted ten years of not being with her, but it was God's timing, and he was determined not to waste another moment. Since they'd been reunited, they had rarely spent an evening apart, other than the week he'd had to return to Florida to take care of his house there. He would either come to her house or she and Jack would come to his apartment for dinner and devotions. On the weekends, they would drive to Keystone and spend the days with Margie and Dan, who seemed to be at the lodge just as often. She didn't know it, but he had planned a magical trip to Hawaii for them for their honeymoon.

Kaitlyn stepped onto the podium under the gazebo they'd had built, handed her bouquet to Melody, and took Dillon's hands. "You are a vision," he whispered.

"You're not so bad yourself," she mouthed back.

"Dearly beloved, we are gathered here today to join these two in holy matrimony," the pastor began. "Kaitlyn and Dillon have been friends for more than a decade. Some of you went to school with them, others watched them grow up. Some of you may have even been around during their first breakup. However, God has a plan for these two, and he has brought them together with a bond even stronger than the first time. Just as a bone is often stronger after it is broken, so sometimes is love because now it has been tested by the flame. Kaitlyn and Dillon have survived that flame and they have chosen to write their own vows today. Dillon?"

Dillon took a deep breath and focused on Kaitlyn's eyes. They were his strength, his sense of calm. "Kaitlyn Bell, from the moment you stepped into my life, you changed me. You made me want to be a better person. For a time, I forgot that and I found myself not liking who I had become, but you gave me a second chance and showed me that love is worth waiting for. The day you agreed to marry me was the happiest day of my life. Until now. And I can't wait to start the rest of my life with you and Jack by my side."

Then it was Kaitlyn's turn. "Dillon Fields, I'm pretty sure I loved you from the moment I met you. You were my rock after I lost my mother, and you accepted all of me with open arms. When you left, it turned my world upside down and I walked some hard paths. I had almost given up on love until you came back into my life. You showed me that love can be renewed and that the best things do come to those who wait. I'm glad we don't have to wait any longer though."

Another small chorus of chuckles scattered through the audience before the pastor spoke again. "Jack, do you have the ring?"

"Do I?" Jack asked loudly. "I've been so careful."

"Will you please hand the ring to Dillon?"

Jack took a step toward Dillon, but as his eyes were so focused on the pillow, he missed the step up and stumbled to the floor sending the ring flying. "NO!"

The pillow landed in front of the pastor, the ring still attached. Jack's eyes grew large. "You mean it was fastened the whole time?"

This time the laughter was louder and Dillon bit his lip to keep from joining in. Kaitlyn's shoulders shook with silent laughter.

Mustering as much dignity as he could, Jack stood, retrieved the pillow, and handed it to Dillon. "Thank you, sir," Dillon said as he pulled the tiny string and freed the ring. Jack shook his head one more time before returning to Grant's side.

"Please repeat after me. I, Dillon, take thee, Kaitlyn, to be my wife. I promise to love you and only you for the rest of my life, forsaking all others. This ring is a symbol of our united love and with it, I thee wed."

Dillon repeated the words and slid the ring on Kaitlyn's finger. Then it was her turn.

"I, Kaitlyn, take thee, Dillon, to be my husband. I promise to love you and only you for the rest of my life, forsaking all others. This ring is a symbol of our united love and with it, I thee wed." She slid his band on and they joined hands once more.

"If there is anyone here who has just cause why these two should not be married, let them speak now or forever hold their peace." Though Dillon expected no objection, he was relieved when the crowd remained silent. "Then by the power vested to me by God and the great state of Colorado, I now pronounce you husband and wife. You may kiss your bride."

Dillon pulled Kaitlyn to him, and though he had kissed her many times before, it felt different kissing her as his wife. He wanted the kiss to last forever, but the sound of applause broke the moment and he pulled back, smiling at the woman he loved. It might have taken ten years, but he had finally returned home. He knew no matter what the future brought, he and Kaitlyn would find a way to weather it together. And he couldn't wait to grow their family.

The end!

If you loved this book, please leave a review. It really does help others find books they'll enjoy too.

AUTHOR'S NOTE

Love Renewed was such a joy to write. First, it was amazing to be in a multi-author set with so many other talented authors. I know some of you have asked me when there will be more on Kaitlyn and Dillon, but since this wasn't my series, I have to wait until the Second Chance group decide to write another. They do have plans, but I promise if they don't soon, then I'll create a spin off based on the lodge. I think there could be some exciting stories there.

This book had another friend of mine from the gym appear in it, but I actually had to apologize to him for it. Normally, when I put someone I know as a character in my books, I try to make them out to be the hero or at least a pretty major character who is good. And that was my plan with Julian. But…. halfway through, it wasn't working for

him to be a love interest for Kaitlyn and so he became…
well….creepy. Thankfully, my friend Julien wasn't too
upset. He told me first of all that I spelled his name wrong,
so it wasn't really him. LOL. Then he said he actually liked
being the creepy guy. He so isn't in real life, so I think this
was his way of being someone else.

My Julien is a 6'3" baby-faced, hits as hard as rock, kick
boxer. He is kind to everyone and almost always smiling, so
not like the Julian in the book. Still, it was fun to put a little
mystery in this book. Maybe I'll do some more. Just to be
different.

Speaking of different. I have another book that I think
you will enjoy though it isn't quite a romance. It is guaran-
teed to make you think, and I promise there will be more in
the series soon.

I hope you enjoyed this book. If you did, would you do
me a favor? Please leave a review. It really helps. It doesn't
have to be long - just a few words to help other readers know
what they're getting.

I'd love to hear from you, not only about this story, but
about the characters or stories you'd like read in the future.
I'm always looking for new ideas and if I use one of your
characters or stories, I'll send you a free ebook and paperback of the book with a special dedication. Write to me at
loranahoopes@gmail.com. And if you'd like to see what's
coming next, be sure to stop by authorloranahoopes.com

I also have a weekly newsletter that contains many

wonderful things like pictures of my adorable children, chances to win awesome prizes, new releases and sales I might be holding, great books from other authors, and anything else that strikes my fancy and that I think you would enjoy. I'll even send you the first chapter of my newest (maybe not even released yet) book if you'd like to sign up.

Even better, I solemnly swear to only send out one news-letter a week (usually on Tuesday unless life gets in the way which with three kids it usually does). I will not spam you, sell your email address to solicitors or anyone else, or any of those other terrible things.

This series will be continued, but for now, would you like to meet some characters for a new series.

PRAYERS AND BLESSINGS,

Lorana

NOT READY TO SAY GOODBYE YET?

Kaitlyn and Dillon were fun though it always makes me think of past loves. Come on, I'm not the only one who thinks about how different life would be if they had married a past love, am I?

Anyway, this next book isn't exactly a love story, but it might have some love along the way. It's a book that weighed on me for a year, but I finally finished it. I hope you'll enjoy it even though it's very different from what I normally write.

The Still Small Voice

KAT JENKINS HAD her world rocked when her best friend died...

She's angry at God and lashing out at those she cares about. To make matters worse, she's begun seeing a light around some people. Is she going crazy?

Jordan Wright is just a college student...

Jordan appeared in When Hearts Collide, but now she gets her own story. After giving up her son for adoption, she's turned her heart to God, but she never expected to receive the gift he's given.

A woman in a window....

Following a vision, Jordan crosses the country, but can she convince Kat that she has a gift and a purpose?

Read on for a taste of The Still Small Voice....

THE STILL SMALL VOICE PREVIEW

"**K**at, honey, what are you doing?" Leah had just laid her two-year old daughter down for the night, but the girl kept tilting her head to look around Leah.

"Trying to see Jesus." Kat smiled matter-of-factly as she looked up at the ceiling. As if this were a common occurrence.

Leah followed her gaze but all she saw was the smoke detector attached to the ceiling. "I don't see anything, honey."

"Jesus is right there, Mommy. Don't you see him?" Kat's green eyes were wide and round beneath her dark curls.

"I don't honey." Leah tried to keep her voice even as she shook her head. She didn't want her daughter to know she was afraid of her seeing visions. This wasn't the first time she had claimed to see Jesus.

The first time, Jesus had been on the hall ceiling as they were heading out to church.

"Are you ready, munchkin?" Leah scooped up her daughter who giggled as she flew through the air. "You ready to go to church?"

Kat's curls bobbed as she nodded.

"And do you love Jesus?"

Kat's tiny mouth pulled into a large smile and she pointed to the corner of the ceiling. "Uh huh. Hi, Jesus." She waved her little hand, the same way she waved to Leah whenever she dropped her off with the nanny.

Leah brushed it off as a two-year old's imagination. "Do you see Jesus up there?" Kat nodded again and Leah kissed her on the cheek. "Well, that's nice. I wish I could see Jesus like you do."

The second time, Jesus appeared in the corner of Kat's ceiling as Leah was reading her a story.

"Honey, where are you going? The story isn't finished yet."

Leah watched as Kat toddled over to the small area between the closed bedroom door and the closet. She pointed her tiny hand up at the ceiling. "Hi, Jesus." Then she held up her bunny as if offering the stuffed toy to someone. "No?" She lowered the bunny and looked around the room.

Then she grabbed a book, returned to the spot, and held it up. "No? Okay." She returned to Leah and climbed back onto her lap to finish the story. "He doesn't want bunny."

Leah forced a tight-lipped smile across her face. Was her daughter really seeing Jesus or was this the natural young child imagination at work?

Tonight, Jesus was in a different place. He was still on the ceiling but now firmly over the foot of Kat's bed instead of by her bedroom door. While Leah hoped her daughter was seeing Jesus, she couldn't dismiss the possibility that she was seeing something else and that bothered her. "Can you tell me what he looks like?"

"He's wearing white, but he's not talking to Bunny." Kat held up her stuffed bunny – the one that went everywhere with her. Once a soft pink color, time and dirt had worn the plush animal to a dull grey color now.

"Does he talk to you?" Leah supposed she should be relieved that whatever Kat was seeing was wearing white and not black, but the fact he didn't talk struck her as odd. If Kat was seeing Jesus, wouldn't He tell her how much He loved her or something like that? Leah was a religious person. She believed in God, but she'd never seen God or heard Him speak to her.

"He's not talking right now."

"Is he smiling?" She was trying not to ask leading questions, but it was hard with a two-year-old who was just now putting sentences together. Leah wished she could see what her daughter was seeing to make sure it was safe.

"Mommy, who's that?"

Leah followed the tiny index finger pointing to the top of Kat's closet. "I don't know, honey. I don't see anything." A cold stone settled in Leah's stomach. It was one thing to be seeing Jesus, but now she was seeing something else too? What was wrong with her daughter? She tried to keep the tremor out of her voice as she spoke again. "Here, let's get to sleep. We'll see Jesus in the morning."

She whipped the blanket up and let it fall until it covered Kat completely, another thing Leah found odd. Most of her friends said their children were afraid of the dark, but Kat wanted to be under the blanket. It had to cover her head and her toes. Leah wondered if the visions were why Kat wanted her head covered. Though not simultaneous, they had started at similar times.

Leah sat in the rocker in Kat's room until she heard the rhythmic cadence of breathing signaling her sleep; then she tiptoed out of the room and to the master bedroom down the hall. Her Bible lay on her nightstand, where she kept it to remind her to read every night, and she picked it up before sinking to her knees on the floor.

She clutched the Bible against her chest and turned her head heavenward. "Lord, please protect my daughter. I don't know what she is seeing, but please protect her." That was all Leah could get out before the tears ran down her cheeks. She had waited so long for her baby girl, and now she was terrified that either something was wrong with her or that something would happen to her.

Continue reading The Still Small Voice....

A FREE STORY FOR YOU

E njoyed this story? Not ready to quit reading yet? If you sign up for my newsletter, you will receive The Billionaire's Impromptu Bet right away as my thank you gift for choosing to hang out with me.

The Billionaire's Impromptu Bet

A SWAT officer. A bored billionaire heiress. A bet that could change everything….

Read on for a taste of The Billionaire's Impromptu Bet….

THE BILLIONAIRE'S IMPROMPTU BET
PREVIEW

Brie Carter fell back spread eagle on her queen-sized canopy bed sending her blond hair fanning out behind her. With a large sigh, she uttered, "I'm bored."

"How can you be bored? You have like millions of dollars." Her friend, Ariel, plopped down in a seated position on the bed beside her and flicked her raven hair off her shoulder. "You want to go shopping? I hear Tiffany's is having a special right now."

Brie rolled her eyes. Shopping? Where was the excitement in that? With her three platinum cards, she could go shopping whenever she wanted. "No, I'm bored with shopping too. I have everything. I want to do something exciting. Something we don't normally do."

Brie enjoyed being rich. She loved the unlimited credit

cards at her disposal, the constant apparel of new clothes, and of course the penthouse apartment her father paid for, but lately, she longed for something more fulfilling.

Ariel's hazel eyes widened. "I know. There's a new bar down on Franklin Street. Why don't we go play a little game?"

Brie sat up, intrigued at the secrecy and the twinkle in Ariel's eyes. "What kind of game?"

"A betting game. You let me pick out any man in the place. Then you try to get him to propose to you."

Brie wrinkled her nose. "But I don't want to get married." She loved her freedom and didn't want to share her penthouse with anyone, especially some man.

"You don't marry him, silly. You just get him to propose."

Brie bit her lip as she thought. It had been awhile since her last relationship and having a man dote on her for a month might be interesting, but…. "I don't know. It doesn't seem very nice."

"How about I sweeten the pot? If you win, I'll set you up on a date with my brother."

Brie cocked her head. Was she serious? The only thing Brie couldn't seem to buy in the world was the affection of Ariel's very handsome, very wealthy, brother. He was a movie star, just the kind of person Brie could consider marrying in the future. She'd had a crush on him as long as she and Ariel had been friends, but he'd always seen her as just that, his little sister's friend. "I thought you didn't want me dating your brother."

"I don't." Ariel shrugged. "But he's between girlfriends right now, and I know you've wanted it for ages. If you win this bet, I'll set you up. I can't guarantee any more than one date though. The rest will be up to you."

Brie wasn't worried about that. Charm she possessed in abundance. She simply needed some alone time with him, and she was certain she'd be able to convince him they were meant to be together. "All right. You've got a deal."

Ariel smiled. "Perfect. Let's get you changed then and see who the lucky man will be.

A tiny tug pulled on Brie's heart that this still wasn't right, but she dismissed it. This was simply a means to an end, and he'd never have to know.

JESSE CALHOUN RELAXED as the rhythmic thudding of the speed bag reached his ears. Though he loved his job, it was stressful being the SWAT sniper. He hated having to take human lives and today had been especially rough. The team had been called out to a drug bust, and Jesse was forced to return fire at three hostiles. He didn't care that they fired at his team and himself first. Taking a life was always hard, and every one of them haunted his dreams.

"You gonna bust that one too?" His co-worker Brendan

appeared by his side. Brendan was the opposite of Jesse in nearly every way. Where Jesse's hair was a dark copper, Brendan's was nearly black. Jesse sported paler skin and a dusting of freckles across his nose, but Brendan's skin was naturally dark and freckle free.

Jesse flashed a crooked grin, but kept his eyes on the small, swinging black bag. The speed bag was his way to release, but a few times he had started hitting while still too keyed up and he had ruptured the bag. Okay, five times, but who was counting really? Besides, it was a better way to calm his nerves than other things he could choose. Drinking, fights, gambling, women.

"Nah, I think this one will last a little longer." His shoulders began to burn, and he gave the bag another few punches for good measure before dropping his arms and letting it swing to a stop. "See? It lives to be hit at least another day." Every once in a while, Jesse missed training the way he used to. Before he joined the force, he had been an amateur boxer, on his way to being a pro, but a shoulder injury had delayed his training and forced him to consider something else. It had eventually healed, but by then he had lost his edge.

"Hey, why don't you come drink with us?" Brendan clapped a hand on Jesse's shoulder as they headed into the locker room.

"You know I don't drink." Jesse often felt like the outsider of the team. While half of the six-man team was married, the other half found solace in empty bottles and meaningless relationships. Jesse understood that - their job was such that they never knew if they would come home night after night - but he still couldn't partake.

Brendan opened his locker and pulled out a clean shirt. He peeled off his current one and added deodorant before tugging on the new one. "You don't have to drink. Look, I won't drink either. Just come and hang out with us. You have no one waiting for you at home."

That wasn't entirely true. Jesse had Bugsy, his Boston Terrier, but he understood Brendan's point. Most days, Jesse went home, fed Bugsy, made dinner, and fell asleep watching TV on the couch. It wasn't much of a life. "All right, I'll go, but I'm not drinking."

Brendan's lips pulled back to reveal his perfectly white teeth. He bragged about them, but Jesse knew they were veneers. "That's the spirit. Hurry up and change. We don't want to leave the rest of the team waiting."

"Is everyone coming?" Jesse pulled out his shower necessities. Brendan might feel comfortable going out with just a new application of deodorant, but Jesse needed to wash more than just dirt and sweat off. He needed to wash the sound of the bullets and the sight of lifeless bodies from his mind.

"Yeah, Pat's wife is pregnant again and demanding some crazy food concoctions. Pat agreed to pick them up if she let him have an hour. Cam and Jared's wives are having a girls' night, so the whole gang can be together. It will be nice to hang out when we aren't worried about being shot at."

"Fine. Give me ten minutes. Unlike you, I like to clean up before I go out."

Brendan smirked. "I've never had any complaints. Besides, do you know how long it takes me to get my hair like this?"

Jesse shook his head as he walked into the shower, but he knew it was true. Brendan had rugged good looks and muscles to match. He rarely had a hard time finding a woman. Jesse on the other hand hadn't dated anyone in the last few months. It wasn't that he hadn't been looking, but he was quieter than his teammates. And he wasn't looking for right now. He was looking for forever. He just hadn't found it yet.

Click here to continue reading The Billionaire's Impromptu Bet.

THE STORY DOESN'T END!

You've met a few people and fallen in love....

I bet you're wondering how you can meet everyone else.

Star Lake Series:

Sealed with a Kiss: Meet the quirky cast of Star Lake and find out if Max and Layla will ever find love.

When Love Returns: Return to Star Lake to hear Presley's story and find out if she gets the second chance with her first love.

Once Upon a Star: Continue the journey when aspiring actress Audrey returns home with a baby. Will Blake finally get the nerve to share his feelings with her?

Love Conquers All: Meet Lanie Perkins Hall who never imagined being divorced at thirty or falling for an old friend, but will his secrets keep them apart?

The Star Lake Collection: Get the latter three stories in one place. Series will include book 1 when it releases around November 2020.

Patriot Peak:

Her Second Chance: When a ghost from Merribeth's past threatens her son, nothing is more important than saving the people that Chance can't keep out of his heart.

Her First Love: A veteran who wants to settle down and start a family. A woman with a secret that could destroy everything.

The Heartbeats Series:

Where It All Began: Sandra Baker finds forgiveness and healing even after making a horrible choice.

The Power of Prayer: Will Callie Green find true love or be defined by her mistake?

When Hearts Collide: When Amanda Adams goes to college, she finds a world she was not ready for. But will she also find true love?

A Past Forgiven: Jess Peterson has lived a life of abuse and lost her self worth, but when she finds herself pregnant, will she find new hope?

The Heartbeats Collection: Grab all four Heartbeats novels in one collection

Sweet Billionaires Series:

The Billionaire's Impromptu Bet: Can a spoiled rich girl change when a bet turns to love?

The Billionaire's Secret: Can a playboy settle down

when he finds out he has a daughter who needs him?

A Brush with a Billionaire: What happens when a stuck up actor lands in a small town and needs help from a female mechanic?

The Billionaire's Christmas Miracle: A twist on a Cinderella story when a billionaire meets a woman who doesn't belong at the ball.

The Billionaire's Cowboy Groom: Will one night six years ago keep Carrie from finding true love?

The Cowboy Billionaire: Can a small town soften the heart of the man sent to buy her ranch?

The Billionaire's Bliss: This collection contains The Billionaire's Secret, The Billionaire's Christmas Miracle, and The Billionaire's Cowboy Groom

The Lawkeeper Series:

Lawfully Matched: When the man she agreed to marry turns out to have a dark past, will Kate have to return home or will she find love with her rescuer in this historical fiction?

Lawfully Justified: Can a bounty hunter and a widow find love together in this historical fiction?

The Scarlet Wedding: William and Emma are planning their wedding, but an outbreak and a return from his past force them to change their plans. Is a happily ever after still in their future in this historical fiction?

Lawfully Redeemed: What happens when a K9 cop falls for the brother of her suspect? Contemporary romance.

The Lawkeeper Collection: Get all four books in one collection

The Are You Listening Series:

The Still Small Voice: Will Jordan listen to God's prompting in this speculative fiction?

A Spark in the Darkness Will Jordan be able to help Raven before the rapture occurs?

The Beginning of the End: After the believers disappear, Raven is left trying to spread the word of God, but a pandemic threatens her progress.

Faith Over Fear: The stunning conclusion to the series.

Blushing Brides Series:

The Cowboy's Reality Bride: He's agreed to be the bachelor on a reality dating show, but what happens when he falls for a woman who's not one of the contestants?

The Reality Bride's Baby: Laney wants nothing more than a baby, but when she starts feeling dizzy is it pregnancy or something more serious?

The Producer's Unlikely Bride: What happens when a producer and an author agree to a fake relationship?

Ava's Blessing in Disguise: Five years after marriage, Ava faces a mysterious illness that threatens to ruin her career. Will she find out what it is?

The Soldier's Steadfast Bride: It was just a pretend pact between children. Wasn't it?

The Men of Fire Beach

Fire Games: Cassidy returns home from Who Wants to

Marry a Cowboy to find obsessive letters from a fan. The cop assigned to help her wants to get back to his case, but what she sees at a fire may just be the key he's looking for.

Lost Memories and New Beginnings: A doctor, a patient with no memory, the men out to get her. Can he keep her safe when he doesn't know who he's looking for?

When Questions Abound: A Companion story to Lost Memories. Told from Detective Graves' point of view.

Never Forget the Past: Fireman Bubba must confront his past in order to clear his name and save lives.

Love on the Run: Graham is forced into lockdown with one of his employees. Will he be able to save her from her ex and will she steal his heart?

Secrets and Suspense: Cara Hunter is hiding something about her military past. When she's suspected of murder, will she be able to convince Cole she's the victim?

Rescue My Heart: Al's sister has gone missing. Will she find her in time?

The Men of Fire Beach Collection: Books 1-3

Texas Tornadoes

Defending My Heart: Forced to confront his past, Emmitt finds news that will change his life.

Run With My Heart: Sentenced to community service, Tucker finds himself falling for the manager.

Love on the Line: Blaine has hired Kenzi to redo his cabin, but what happens when she finds his darkest secret?

Touchdown on Love: When Mason's injury throws him

together with ex-girlfriend, will sparks fly again?

Second Chance Reception: Jefferson is hiding something. When he falls for the team cook, will he let her in?

A Divine Interception: Can Carter and April find love?

Small Town Short Stories

Small Town Dreams

Small Town Second Chances

Small Town Rivals

Small Town Life

Life in a Small Town: All four stories in one collection

Stand Alones:

Love Renewed: This books is part of the multi author second chance series. When fate reunites high school sweethearts separated by life's choices, can they find a second chance at love at a snowy lodge amid a little mystery?

Her children's early reader chapter book series:

The Wishing Stone #1: Dangerous Dinosaur

The Wishing Stone #2: Dragon Dilemma

The Wishing Stone #3: Mesmerizing Mermaids

The Wishing Stone #4: Pyramid Puzzle

The Wishing Stone: Mary's Miracle

The Wishing Stone Collection

To see a list of all her books

authorloranahoopes.org

loranahoopes@gmail.com

ABOUT THE AUTHOR

Lorana Hoopes is a USA Today Best selling inspirational author originally from Texas but now living in the PNW with her husband and three children. When not writing, she can be seen kickboxing at the gym, singing, or acting on stage. One day, she hopes to retire from teaching and write full time.